MW01670821

TYRANNOSAURUS TUNDRA

SAM M. PHILLIPS

SEVEREDPRESS

TYRANNOSAURUS TUNDRA

Copyright © 2026 Sam M. Phillips

WWW.SEVEREDPRESS.COM

All rights reserved. No part of this book may be reproduced or transmitted in any form or by any electronic or mechanical means, including photocopying, recording or by any information and retrieval system, without the written permission of the publisher and author, except where permitted by law. This novel is a work of fiction. Names, characters, places and incidents are the product of the author's imagination, or are used fictitiously. Any resemblance to actual events, locales or persons, living or dead, is purely coincidental.

ISBN: 978-1-923663-29-9

All rights reserved.

1

Leo looks into the unblinking eyes of the dinosaur. The black slits of its pupils stare back, irises like solar flares radiating tendrils of iridescent yellow and orange. They are the eyes of a killer.

A bead of sweat slides down Leo's temple. His hands tremble and he nearly drops what he's holding. His stiff fingers grip it firmly once more, heart beating, fearful of fumbling the precious object. He resists the urge to glance at it and keeps his attention on the dinosaur, transfixed by its hypnotic gaze.

With his other hand he reaches out, groping blindly on the desk for what he needs. There is a clattering tinkle of scattered wooden handles as he tips over a mug. He curses, breaking the mesmerising spell of the dinosaur to find what he's after. Sorting through the handles quickly, he mumbles the numbers printed on their sides as he seeks the right one. Pinching the thin length of wood in nervous fingers, he returns to studying the dinosaur in detail.

The creature still stares, and though it is merely an illustration, its eyeballs flicker with a touch of life as the glossy page of the reference book catches the light of the desk's fluorescent lamp. Leo feels the accusation in that glassy gaze, that he will never replicate the stunning beauty of such delicate sensory instruments, perfected by evolution.

Still, he knows he must try, and so he lifts both hands together like a conductor beginning a symphony. In one, he grips the handle of the tiny paintbrush taken from the mug. In the other is the precious scale miniature of his favourite dinosaur, Tyrannosaurus rex. Made of cast resin and meticulously painted by him during the past weeks using acrylic paints, the colours and patterns he's chosen for the model's sculpted scales and skin are taken from the reference book, although he knows even these are mere guesses. Still, it's a lifelike representation, as best as anyone is aware.

Now for the final, delicate touch. He dips the brush in the black paint, just the very tip, taking the most miniscule amount of paint. With his tongue poking between his lips as he concentrates, he hunches forward, holding the small Tyrannosaurus up to the light, and with infinite care, brings the brush to the model's eye, slicing the coloured iris in half with a perfect vertical black line.

He breathes out a breath he didn't know he'd been holding, and leans back to inspect his work, turning the model to see if the eye looks natural. Pleased, he sucks in another breath and holds it as he dips the brush in the paint once more. The tip hovers over the second iris. He has spent many hours perfecting each of these, getting the sunburst patterning and colours just right. He guides the brush in like a surgeon's scalpel, laser focused.

The bead of sweat from his forehead slides down, catching in the corner of his eye and making it twitch. His vision blurs but he blinks it away and continues, so close now. The tip wavers as he fights down his nervousness, not wanting to ruin his model, all his work. He squeezes the brush to steady it, but this only increases the trembling.

It grows worse until it feels like the movement is outside of him. With a violent heave, the whole room lurches to the side, tilting at an angle. The reference book is tossed onto the floor and snaps shut like a set of closing jaws. The mug smashes with a brilliant sound and the paintbrushes skitter everywhere. Leo locks his fingers around the delicate resin dinosaur, but his other hand slips, slashing across the model with a blob of black paint. The room tilts the other way, and Leo drops the brush, grabbing hold of the lamp before it, too, is smashed on the floor.

"Damn waves," he says.

The ship rocks back and forth, Leo's cabin with it, and he waits for it to settle. When it does his eyes are drawn inexorably to the marring line of paint ruining the model. He breathes out an exasperated sigh and places the miniature down, the adhesive putty on its plastic base affixing it to the desk. He bends to pick up the reference book.

"Oh, just perfect," he says as it drips black paint. He turns the gooey pages to find the illustration of the Tyrannosaurus smeared with a fat black line of spillage. He plops the book down on the desk by the model. "I guess they match now, at least."

There is a knock at the door of the cabin.

"Come in," says Leo. The door opens.

It's a young female crew member wearing the same black coveralls as Leo. Above one breast pocket her name is stitched in white thread. Above the other, the stylised silhouette of a Tyrannosaurus head is overlaid across a four-pointed compass rose. This is the logo of the DEP, the Dinosaur Expeditionary Project.

"Captain," she says. Her face is ashen white as if she's seen a ghost, and she's panting hard, fighting to catch her breath.

"What is it?" asks Leo, sitting bolt upright.

"We've been pinged."

***

Leo grabs his heavy, fur-lined jacket from its hook by the door as he exits the room. "Move!" he says, bounding up the stairs three at a time, his boots ringing on steel. The crew member flattens herself against the wall and he squeezes past her in the tight space. Stepping through a bulkhead hatch he clocks his head like he does every time, his height a hindrance on their modestly sized ship.

The *Cretaceous* isn't built for comfort. It's a tough, practical vessel, a repurposed Argentinian patrol ship bought on the cheap, yet able to handle difficult polar conditions. Her short length has its advantages, though, and Leo is on the bridge a few seconds later. He bursts through the door, greeted by a familiar sight.

Crystal clear skies stretch into infinity, reflecting light upon the face of sapphire waters. The Southern Ocean is as hard and dark as this deep blue stone, and yet it undulates with a shifting landscape of waves, its surface like the chest of a colossal monster breathing in and out.

Icebergs the size of skyscrapers float by as if suspended above these rolling hills of water, their tapered sides seeming to leech some of the blueness from sky and sea, infusing them with a glow which adds fine detail to their otherwise uniform white sides. Distorted mirror images of the icebergs play in the water by their bases, suggesting another, inverted world which exists in the depths, quickly washed away in the turbulence of waves crashing against their sides.

It takes Leo's breath away, as it does every time. It also reminds him how damn cold it is in the Antarctic Circle, even in summer, and he throws his jacket on as his breathing mists in the air. His fingers feel numb, and he squeezes his fists tight to reintroduce the circulation.

He always forgets such things when he's lost in his hobby. Painting the dinosaurs takes him away from his worries even as they remind him why he came here. But his worries are close at hand as he tears himself away from the stunning view through the forward windows of the bridge and looks to the faces of the people around him, the crew he's dragged halfway around the world in search of a myth.

They're scared, with lines of strain creasing brows and invisible hooks pulling down at the corners of their mouths. Eyes glitter, as wide and vulnerable as those of animals caught in the light from a hunter's torch. Leo's scans across them, attempting an encouraging smile but only managing a stressed grimace.

His gaze lands upon a particular face, and his daughter Greta gives him a hard, urgent stare back. His pinched expression softens in genuine affection even as hers stretches into a forced leer, her lips a tight slit. He winks at her in reassurance but even this fails to melt the ice in her piercing eyes, blue like her mother's. They dart from him to the instruments of her station before her, and he rushes over, summoned as if by an unspoken command to stare at the screen.

He takes in the information at a glance, the black screen pinging with flares of green light as the dish atop the ship spins to cast its invisible rays across the horizon.

"Something's out there," Greta says.

"Yes," says Leo, looking up to squint through the windows. "And they know where we are."

He scans the horizon, but sees only endless water studded with icebergs, slowly shifting like mountain silhouettes in the background of a puppet show. Waves undulate under the ship, lifting it as if hoisting it on the shoulders of a giant, and Leo catches a glimpse of something dark among the bright shapes. It is sharp, like a blade, and just as threatening. It slips behind an iceberg, disappearing once more like a spectre only glimpsed out of the corner of the eye. He blinks, unsure if his sight is betraying him, or if his mind is making things up. But the ping sounds again and again, ticking like a clock in a countdown, the green line on the screen spinning like an overexcited minute hand, time running fast, and Leo knows it isn't an illusion.

"Patrol ship?" suggests Greta.

Leo gives his head a quick shake like a shiver has climbed up his spine. "They're acting strangely. That's an active ping. They don't care if we know they're out there as long as they pinpoint us."

"Shouldn't they be hailing us on the radio, warning us off like the other times?"

Leo points at the flaring green dot, creeping closer to the centre of the screen with each sweep. "I think we've had our last warning. They're coming for us."

"What do we do?" asks Greta. Her blue eyes flash defiance, pulsing with each flare of light upon the screen.

A bead of sweat rolls down the side of Leo's temple and into his twitching eye. This time the sweat pools there, stinging badly with increased potency, the stakes having been raised exponentially. He can't blink it away. It remains there, festering with poisonous stress.

He looks around at the scared faces, sees his own fear mirrored there. The pinging grows more frequent, the hunter looming just beyond sight, yet closing for the kill. Leo wipes his hand through the tight curls of his beard, smearing saliva from the corners of his mouth across dry lips.

"I need time to think, damn it," he says, but he doesn't have time. Choices are being forced upon him. He can't turn and fight. The *Cretaceous* has no weapons, besides a pistol locked in Leo's desk for emergencies. But this is an emergency, and what good is it now? He has only one option.

He turns to Greta.

"We run."

2

The *Cretaceous* bobs and weaves among the ice flows, its engines straining as Leo pushes it to maximum speed. If it were winter they'd be locked in by a thick crust of surface ice, forced to a crawl as they sought places where it was thin enough to crack through with their bow. But it is summer, when the ocean is a moving maze, the ice melting just enough to become mobile.

Small mountains of the stuff shift like slow moving avalanches, pieces cracking off the sides of icebergs and tumbling into the churning waters. Waves heave under the ice, making its white sheet surface sparkle in a dazzling play of moving bands of light as it bulges and sinks. Clear patches of water between are dark, hinting at hidden dangers—submerged ice and other unknown perils—but it's these that Leo aims for, a way through as he constantly looks over his shoulder for a glimpse of their hunter.

Scanning the horizon with binoculars he can't see them, even though he knows they are there. The pings grow more insistent, echoing his racing heartbeat.

"Dad," says Greta, pointing through a window. Leo swings around, aiming the binoculars. In the small world of a pair of circles, a shadow prowls at the edge of an iceberg, a dark triangle which slices the water. It cleaves the edge of an iceberg as it passes, swinging in close as it turns, trying to catch its prey unawares. The ice tumbles into the ocean with a geyser spray of tossed up water. The ship emerges through this scattered mist like a magician in a puff of smoke, no longer a shadow, but a grey length of steel, its bow sharp as a sword pointed at Leo's heart.

"It's barrelling down on us," says Leo, lowering the binoculars. The ship becomes a small dot in the distance, but he can't let the illusion give him comfort. It's moving fast, gunning for them.

Leo turns to the helmsman. "Give it all we've got."

He prays it will be enough.

***

Water explodes off the starboard bow as a weight drops into it. For a second, Leo thinks it's a portion of a crumbling iceberg. The *Cretaceous* is tight in among a number of these. They tower over them on all sides like snowy giants as Leo tries to give their pursuer the shake. More than one close call has sent ice plunging across their deck in showers of scattered, diamond-like chunks as they pass between the shifting labyrinth of icy ravines, pathways opening and closing as icebergs collide and separate unpredictably.

"If we can just get into the slipstream channel by the coast, we'll shoot along it and outpace them," says Leo, more to reassure himself that he's not leading them to disaster, rather than to calm the fears of anyone else. He looks at Greta, and she nods her approval. She knows what the order really means, why the dart for the coast.

"I didn't come this far to not find out," Leo says to her under his breath.

"It's what Mum would have wanted," she says.

"What she would have wanted is to live to see this."

Leo doesn't wait around to see the hurt his words cause, rushing over to the window as another eruption of water spouts into the air. This time he sees the cause, not falling ice, but a dark object, small and fast.

"They're shooting at us," he says, and immediately regrets his words. They cause a panic among the crew.

"Get back to your stations!" Leo barks as a number of them get up to run. They pause, shocked by his tone. Some return, ashamed of their cowardice or cowed by his anger, but others keep moving, as if there's any safety to be found anywhere on the ship.

"I said sit!" shouts Leo, moving towards the door to block it. Standing there, staring down the crew, he understands the temptation to give in to fear. He longs to go to his cabin and hide from his responsibilities. He immediately dismisses this idea, but then another, much darker thought clouds his mind. Retrieve the pistol, maintain order.

"If I need to use that, then I've failed as a leader," he mutters. "I won't give in to fear."

But he already has. It is what brought him here, to the ends of the Earth in search of dinosaurs. Fear of missing out, of not seeing the truth for himself, as his wife will never see, a dream unrealised.

But he can still make it happen. For her. For him. For both of them. There is still time.

But not much.

"Get back to your stations," he says, and is relieved to be obeyed, if reluctantly, by the visibly shaken crew. Leo rushes back to the steering wheel, gripping it tight to still his own trembling hands.

With an echoing bang, followed by a shriek and whine, the pursuers fire again, and Leo winces. The shell strikes the tip of an iceberg as he turns his ship into the lee of its shelter. Ice erupts in a huge explosion, and the iceberg is decapitated, its head falling into the ocean, lifting a huge wave which falls with a loud slap across the deck.

If not for the iceberg, the shell would have struck the ship, and Leo knows the next might end them if he can't find a way out of the ice maze. He makes a snap judgement at a fork in the path, unable to see beyond the bend of the sheer sides of the huddled icebergs, which wheeze and groan as they grind together. Hauling at the wheel, the nose of the *Cretaceous* comes about like a pointing finger of fate. They dart down the fork and around the bend.

"Oh, God, no," breathes Leo, seeing he has chosen wrong. They are trapped, a dead end formed by the bulk of icebergs. There's no way to barge their way through such a thick wall. The ship would crumple like a can. It is dark in this artificial ravine, the dark shroud of impending death falling upon all on the ship as they travel in the shadow of the looming icebergs.

"Take the wheel," Leo says to Greta. He rushes out of the bridge onto the deck and looks down along the length of the rail. The other ship enters the far end of the ravine, a cork pushed into the bottle, sealing their doom. It is an evil-looking thing, a bulky steel robot muscling its way down the tight ravine, inhuman in its cold, sterile lines, unstoppable in its power.

It is a battleship, flying no flag, and with no insignia or markings painted on its hull. It is a phantom, come to destroy all who dare trespass within this final, forbidden circle which girdles this region of Antarctica.

There is no sign of life aboard the battleship, only the motion of turning prow guns, well-oiled gears silent and ominous as they slide the weapon to bear upon the *Cretaceous*. Leo stares down the pair of barrels, dark circles which stare back like baleful eyes.

He blinks as they flare an angry red. A split second later the bang strikes his ears like a blow, staggering him. He slips on the icy deck and tumbles hard onto his ass as the shell screams along the length of his ship. It takes out the radar dish in a shower of sparks and keeps going. Hunks of tortured and distressed metal fall upon the deck, lethal shrapnel which embeds itself even in hardened steel.

Another explosion. The shell strikes the ice wall in front of the *Cretaceous*. Ice crumbles to powder, an avalanche of snow sliding into the ocean with a gigantic splash which sends a huge wave down the length of the ravine. Both ships are lifted, tilted first towards the sky, and then they lower their heads like bowing courtiers, riding down the far side of the wave.

The surge of water throws off the next shot of the battleship, made almost point-blank as it looms close. The singing projectile strikes the icebergs once more with a percussive bang, this time gouging a huge chunk from one, a terrible wound from which it recoils as if in pain, sliding away to create a gap between it and its neighbour.

Like a sign from God, a slither of light shines through this space, piercing Leo's heart with a painful stab of hope. More hunks of ice break loose. They tumble into the water, churning the surface to white froth. The *Cretaceous* ploughs on through this maelstrom, a wounded beast desperate to escape, clawing and scraping the ice to break free through this meagre opening.

"Go," urges Leo, willing Greta at the helm to stay the course, to have courage and push through. The hull of the ship shrieks like nails on a chalkboard as it grinds between the pinch point, the colossal bulk of the icebergs rising like guardian pillars of a gate through which they must pass. Leo offers a silent prayer for his ship to squeeze through, shaking his pressed-together hands to beseech these icy gods for their blessing.

Beneath his feet, the deck vibrates, the engines screaming as Greta forces them beyond their limits. The sound is echoed by the cries of terror and exhilaration from the crew in the bridge, and Leo joins in, unsure if he is witnessing the last moment of his life, or the first of a new beginning which starts just beyond this shifting barrier.

The hull is squeezed as if in a vice, and it almost grinds to a halt. It flexes, more like rubber than steel, then jolts forward, extruded like a sausage through a grinder. Leo yelps with joy as a world of white light washes over him from beyond the gap. But their passing has destabilised the fragile icebergs further. They shudder and groan in complaint. Great chunks of ice break off and rain upon the deck.

Leo's cry of triumph is choked off in his throat as a giant frozen spear nearly impales him. He jumps back, startled, his reflexes too slow if it were to have hit him, and the huge shard of ice shatters on the deck, peppering his skin painfully with smaller fragments of frozen shrapnel.

Goaded by the pain, he runs towards the shelter of the bridge, eyes turned up to gauge the trajectory of further natural projectiles. They glitter in the sunlight as they fall, tumbling end over end to smash on the deck all around him, each large enough to flatten him. They dent and buckle the deck, and one skitters as it disintegrates, the pieces chasing him through the doorway of the bridge like oversized hail. They get under Leo's feet, sending him tumbling into welcome arms.

"We're through!" says Greta, holding him up with surprising strength. She beams him a smile. Leo smiles back, the relief of the moment overpowering any wider considerations of the danger they're still in. Yet he dares to let himself believe they have escaped. He rushes to the windows, looking back.

The battleship tries to follow, ramming the gap with its bulk. But where the smaller *Cretaceous* was able to squeeze through, the larger ship is wedged tight as if between monstrous boulders. With a terrible squealing like that of an injured whale, it is crushed like a can as the icebergs capriciously change their courses and push inwards once more. Its hull tears and water rushes in through the holes, but it doesn't sink. Instead, it rises and falls like a floating corpse, held in place by the grip of the icebergs.

Only now does Leo see life aboard its twisted deck, tiny figures scuttling for safety in an impossible situation. He considers for a fleeting moment turning back to help them, as he himself would want to be helped in distress, but he shakes this off as he remembers what they tried to do to him.

"It was either us or them," he says, bowing to the brutal realities of the situation.

"At least we know we're on the right track," says Greta. "They wouldn't be so desperate to sink us if they weren't hiding something."

"Not just something, Greta. The greatest secret in the world," says Leo, turning to look across the water, to where the icy walls of the coast of Antarctica rise, brooding and forbidding, yet tantalising in their promise.

***

When the next attack comes, there is no warning. It comes out of a clear, blue sky. But there is a delay between the release of the bombs from the stealth airplanes, high in the stratosphere, and when they strike the tiny, repurposed ship of the DEP.

In this brief moment of realised expectations and unknown dangers, Leo and Greta are truly happy, blissfully unaware of their fate as they stand on the deck of the *Cretaceous*. Their eyes glisten with emotion, turned towards the precious objects of all their years of dreaming and striving.

"It's real," says Leo in hushed awe. Greta reaches out and squeezes her father's quivering hand.

"Mum knew," she says.

"Yes."

Embedded in the ice walls of the Antarctic coastline, arrayed like wax sculptures in a natural history museum, are perfectly preserved dinosaurs. The ship glides along slowly, giving them time to study each in detail across the railing, so close they can almost reach out and touch them.

"They seem so… alive," says Greta, and Leo has to admit it is so, the eyes of the dinosaurs seeming to watch them back, sparkling like glass beads in the sun, as if the ice age had caught them unawares only yesterday, or last month, rather than millions of years ago.

"Aww, triceratops," says Greta, pointing at the wondrous tri-horns.

"Magnificent," says Leo.

"And ankylosaurus. Mum would have loved this."

Tears well in Leo's eyes. "That was her favourite. She liked the clubbed tail."

"Do you know my favourite?" asks Greta.

"The brontosaurus?"

"Maybe when I was twelve, Dad! I'm grown up now."

"I know." He smiles at her. "Your mother would be so proud of you. Do you know *my* favourite?"

"That's not difficult. Tyrannosaurus rex."

"Yes, I don't suppose that was a hard one," Leo says with a chuckle. "I don't see one here, unfortunately." He frowns. "Though there is a stegosaurus."

"Wouldn't be the same without a stegosaurus."

"Yes, but all these others—the triceratops, the ankylosaurus, even the parasaurolophus I can glimpse there in the back through the frost—they're all from the late Cretaceous."

"As is only fitting. Probably why Mum made you promise to christen the ship that."

Leo grunts, dubious of this. The clues which led them to this semi-mythical place were vague, little more than rumours, with few solid details. He and his wife had acted more on faith than fact in their quest, driven by their passion for dinosaurs. And where dinosaurs are concerned, he knows his stuff.

"Stegosaurus is the odd one out," he says. "It's from the late Jurassic. They shouldn't be side by side with these others. There should be strata separating different ages."

"So, what does it mean?"

"I don't know."

Leo scratches his chin, thinking. His eyes drift to the sky, where he catches a glimpse of movement in his peripheral vision. But it's gone before he can turn his head to see what it is.

A whistling sound quietly buzzes deep in his ears like tinnitus. He shoves his pinkie finger down deep into one of them, gives it a shake. The noise not only persists but grows in intensity.

"What's that?" asks Greta, also looking up.

"Oh, you hear it too?"

There is a flash of something small and dark falling, far too fast for their eyes to follow.

Then the *Cretaceous* is struck amidships, and it, along with Leo and Greta, are consumed in a massive, explosive fireball.

3

Standing on an icy coastal cliff, the fierce polar winds whipping his layered clothes, Roman watches a disaster unfold. The ship, similar in design to those the Argentinians use to patrol their sector, is on fire. A huge plume of oily black smoke rises like a distress signal from the ruined deck, fierce flames flickering at its heart. But no one is coming to rescue the people on board.

They're already dead.

Consumed by the fire, their ashes rise with the smoke. These flutter and toss as they're caught by the strong winds, scattering across the water along with the burning pieces of debris which float among the ice flows like the campfires of an already defeated army.

The hull of the ship slouches low; it's taking on water. Soon it will disappear beneath the waves, and in time, when the merciless winter comes, the water will freeze over, burying the wreck forever, the people with it, and it will be like they never existed.

Roman can relate. It's how he feels too.

***

An icy chill runs down Roman's spine. It's not just the biting cold, intense despite the blinding sunshine. Seeing those people killed reminds him of unpleasant realities, things he is trying to forget by coming here to look at the water. Instead of being reminded of the beauty and serenity of nature, using it to escape from his limited world, he sees the wide expanse of the Southern Ocean for what it really is, a moat keeping people out of an impregnable fortress of snow and ice.

"And keeping people in," he says to himself, or perhaps to his companions, though they can't understand him. The emperor penguins honk, their yellow and white chests vibrating as if laughing at a joke. Which, Roman realises, perhaps he is to them, and they gather around him on his walks only to mock him.

It's easy to understand their haughty pride and regal bearing. They're not limited, not like him. They freely come and go.

Roman's wandering, on the other hand, is constricted. There is an invisible barrier only a few metres in front of him he cannot cross, but which they can.

As if to illustrate this point, one of them leans forward and dives from the shallow ledge of the cliff, plunging into the freezing cold water. Like a pack of lemmings, the others shuffle to the edge and jump off, a tumbling mass of sleek charcoal-backed bodies, one after another, entering the ocean with the tight splashes of expert divers.

Roman cannot join them, much as he wants to, for to do so is to die, killed by the cold, and if not that, then by some similar fate as those aboard that ship. The emperor penguins, however, are at home in the water. They swim and twirl beneath the waves with elegant grace as they crash against cliffs filled with the frozen corpses of dinosaurs.

Roman is alone again, as he probably always has been. The penguins aren't company, not really. But still, they're the only friends he has.

He turns back to look at the bleak, utilitarian building in which he lives. Its hard lines are at odds with nature, a crude block of artificial materials rammed into the snow and ice. It is a place in which to cling to existence, not living, merely surviving. It brings him no joy as he trudges across the ice towards it.

***

The walk is a long one. Distances are deceptive in Antarctica, the near-uniform whiteness of the place disrupting depth perception. Even the grey rocks of distant mountains meld into the tundra before them, looking as much like deep ravines cut into the ground as heights rising from it. The optical illusion is completed by the infusion of blue ice which runs through everything like veins in marble, describing chaotic patterns which lead the eyes around in crazed circles, unable to lock onto any solid landmark in nature. Only manmade structures give any context to wide expanses, sticking out like festering sores.

Otherwise, the Antarctic tundra is a flat, infinite plain of permafrost, resembling a barren desert of snow and ice more than any other geographical landscape. It is also a dry place, with less rainfall than the Sahara. Despite, or more accurately because of, the abundance of water frozen as ice, there is little mobile fresh water. Any precipitation falls as snow, and drinking water comes from melting gathered ice.

What other water there is, and this there is in abundance, is greedily hoarded by the ocean which rings the whole continent. There it is poisoned with salt, making the Southern Ocean an inhospitable place of death, an illusionary mirage which resembles a watery oasis. But it is a mere extension of the tundra, an infinite expanse of barren territory.

And yet in between these two places, tundra and ocean, each hostile to life, which Roman must live his life, stuck, as it were, between a rock and hard place, slowly being ground to death, unable to escape.

***

The tundra is not without its wonders. Roman walks across one of them now, long immune to its beauty by the repetition of his passing. Beneath his cleated boots, frozen in the translucent ice, are dark shapes. He glances down at one as he passes, but doesn't linger, disinterested. To see one is to see them all. They are the same, repeated over and over in all directions like an army of black dots hidden just beneath the surface.

To anyone else, they are a marvel. To him, they are the reason for his imprisonment here on this continent at the edge of the world. It is enough for him to hate them, but he's numb with cold and the trudging routine of his life. He doesn't feel now the way he does when he's in his room, warm but discontent, able to think clearer.

Blurred by the crystalline ice, the shapes are like his present thoughts, dark shadows which are suggestive of something bigger. Both are monsters which haunt the world, waiting to be unleashed. They long to be freed but are confined in frigid rigidity.

The cleats of his boots scrape the ice over the top of one of these monsters. The marks they leave are like those left by vicious claws. Roman can't see the claws of the creature below the ice. All he can see is the top of its head, a blocky, elongated shape, flaring around the crown and tapering to a blunt snout.

“Velociraptor,” says Roman as if speaking the name of the creature will let him pass it unmolested. And the creature makes no movement, can make no movement. It is locked away, trapped in the ice, confined by Antarctica as surely as Roman.

He keeps walking, his cleats stabbing the ground—*shunk, shunk, shunk*—as he steps over the heads of hundreds of velociraptors. Seen from above, the dinosaurs look like a stampede aimed towards the base, as if coming to attack the humans within in revenge. But they are frozen in time, out of sync with the living, and Roman doesn’t have to worry about them. They can’t hurt him now.

4

"Hey, here he is, back from his walk with his mates," says Brock as Roman enters the cafeteria. Coming from the wet room which acts like an airlock between the chill of outside and the relative warmth of the base, Roman has taken off his cleated boots, as well as the top couple of layers of fur-lined coats and down-filled pants. In just a tracksuit and socks, he feels practically naked. No longer exposed to the brutal elements, he has to put up with the scouring wind of words bellowing from Brock's mouth instead.

"What you talk to the penguins about this time?" the big man says around a mouthful of food. "Trying to get a date with the emperor's daughter?" Brock guffaws at his joke and elbows his neighbour, who pulls away from the over-enthusiastic ribbing.

"I would, but I haven't managed to break the ice yet," says Roman as he passes. The response is automatic, like a routine, and he doesn't bother to look at Brock, or anyone. He has eyes only for the hot food.

Steam rises from a row of heated buffet pans, their contents lit up with that gentle yellow glow of cafeterias everywhere, reminding Roman painfully yet reassuringly of home. His *real* home. Even after years here he can't think of Antarctica as such. It has become his prison, his nightmare, and he dreams of the day he'll leave it and return to Australia.

His shoulders slump as he picks up a tray and plate. He eyes the pans with slight disgust, yet reaches for the serving spoon, driven by the growling of his stomach. He tries to banish any thoughts of home and focus on the present, but it isn't easy. His parents must be worried sick, not knowing what's become of him. How relieved they'll be to see him. They'll hug him and ask him questions he doesn't want to answer; but he won't care because he'll be eating a home-cooked meal rather than the imposter he piles onto his plate, copied day after day from available stores, which are delivered once a year then eked out mercilessly by humourless cooks.

The repetitious diet further erodes the already tenuous concept of time in a place where the sun shines twenty-four hours a day. At least in summer it does, and Roman shivers despite the heat from the trays as he remembers the eternal darkness of three grim winters already endured, dreading the fourth, only months away. Half a year of continuous night and freezing cold. It's enough to send anyone mad.

How many more such winters lie in his future? He has no sentence to complete, for he isn't technically a prisoner. This is his job. One he signed up for, sure, though it is also one he cannot quit. He never thought it would be easy, living and working in Antarctica, but it seemed like a good opportunity for someone straight out of university. After a few years, he figured, he'd collect his pay and go home. But his contract had ended, and he hadn't been aware of the auto-renew clause. They lied to him about that, as well as so much more.

His plate clatters and rattles on his tray as he carries it to a table, his hands shaking. Sitting alone, as far from Brock as physically possible, he massages them for a while to get them to stop. He convinces himself that it's just the cold, and not fear, which has settled into their bones.

The shaking resumes as he picks up his fork, and it is stilled only by his lips clamping down upon the colourless mush, his teeth clicking on the utensil. The meal is bland, his taste buds long inoculated to its familiar flavours and lack thereof. But it is filling, and hot, and it settles into his complaining guts, quietening them for a time, though not his mind, which continues to chatter incessantly, reminding him of everything he must forget.

***

Brock chases him out of the cafeteria with another verbal broadside after they bus their trays, but Roman doesn't hear, nor does he need the words of others to taunt him. He has his own harsh internal critic. With the cold and hunger now forgotten, his worries crowd at the forefront of his mind. He takes the steps up to the dorm three at a time, frantic for some relief from the chattering voices. Just touching the key to the lock of his room gives a phantom feeling of release, knowing in a moment he'll be away from the others. A cold sweat of anticipation breaks out at the base of his back.

But, closing the door behind him with an ominous click, he realises he hasn't escaped. He's now locked in with his thoughts, which boom louder than ever. The room, far from being a sanctuary, is nothing more than a cell. And there is only one way out. He rummages in his desk drawer for the small bag—how much he had to trade for even this tiny quantity—and pulls it out.

There are precious few of the tiny gummies remaining inside, but he needs one now. Tomorrow, as much as such things can be measured in this hell of eternal daytime, is a problem he'll have to deal with when it comes… if it comes. Scared and anxious, he stuffs one of the gummies in his mouth and chews frantically. Swallowing, he sits on the edge of his bed and stares vacantly at the wall while he waits for it to kick in.

He pictures the emperor penguins, tilting forward to dive headfirst into the icy water, and he imagines joining them. It would be an escape, of sorts, but it's hard to imagine the harsh reality of it—his body cold as a corpse as it sinks—while sitting in his room, with a smooth warmth slowly suffusing through his body.

He slumps down onto the bed, shaking his head. The penguins shake their heads, too. He can see them clearer now. They pop out like three-dimensional pictures, with front and side angles printed on a cube held close to his face. He tilts his head and the cube tilts. It's like looking at a fish in a fish tank, and as he rotates his head, the two-dimensional images of the penguins on the cube's faces shift like an optical illusion. Squinting, trying to piece together the images into a three-dimensional whole, he realises it is impossible, so he tries to wait it out a while.

But he can't wait too long. His shift is starting soon. He looks at his watch. It lies to him, the hands spinning dizzyingly. He looks back at the penguins. They lie too. They're not real. They're photos on printed posters attached to the wall of his room, and he's inside the cube with them; they looking in and him looking out. Why did he bring them inside, with their snowy landscapes reminding him of the grim realities outside?

"Because Brock is right," he says, breaking the spell enough to sit up with a stiff lurch like the risen dead. "They're my only friends."

5

The effect of the gummy, far from impeding him, makes it easier for Roman to go to work, because he has no thoughts to hinder him, and his actions are done on autopilot, long engrained into muscle memory through repetitious drudgery. He doesn't remember travelling to the ice cave, but he does remember the journey from many past experiences, taking the snowmobile across the tundra to the latest dig site, then the cable car lowering him into the dark abyss burrowed into the ice.

Stomping along the length of the cave is like being inside some huge worm that has been caught in a blizzard and frozen solid. He shines his high-powered lamp about. On the walls are colourful outlines, like a caveman's paintings he has come to study. Roman has to blink to bring them into focus and see them for what they are.

Dinosaurs.

But these are not drawings. Like the velociraptors, they are the real thing, frozen inside the walls. Also like the velociraptors, they long ago ceased to rouse any feeling in Roman beside the mundanity of a monotonous task. He checks his manifesto against the numbers carved into the ice beside individual dinosaurs.

"What the hell?" he says, rubbing a section of the wall clear of a gathered layer of frosty rime. It comes away as slush in his glove. He stares at this for a moment in surprise, and then at the number revealed beneath. Its groves, normally deeply and neatly carved, are shallow, with smoothed edges as if filled with flowing meltwater which has once again frozen.

"I can't make it out. Is that a three or an eight?" he says to no one. He used to have a partner to work with. No more, though it's unclear to Roman who broke off the arrangement. In the distance, he can hear the *chink, chink, chink* of other work parties chipping away at the ice, and the burbling echoes of their voices as they talk, occasionally rising to bursting bubbles of laughter which bounce around the icy tunnel's walls, as if the cave itself is mocking him.

Shaking his head, Roman trudges to the next dinosaur, and the next. Each time, it is the same, the numbers obscured, so that his only option is to go back to the start of the tunnel and count off the individual dinosaurs until he finds his assigned workstation for the day.

Doing this takes far too long, the going slow and the dinosaurs far apart, and by the time he's ascertained which he's to work on, he can't hear the voices anymore. The others have finished and left him behind. But he can't return to the base without a sample. One more writeup and he'll be on punishment duty, or worse.

"Though what could be worse than this?" he says, his breath misting in the powerful beam of the lamp. His mind has a ready answer. He suddenly feels claustrophobic in the tunnel, the walls pressing in like those of his room back at base.

He looks up at the looming bulk of the dinosaur set a foot deep into the wall, a shadowy silhouette partially hidden by the frosted ice as if seen through the door of a supermarket freezer. Playing his light across it brings the creature to view in stunning detail, section by section, the sparkling of the ice creating the illusion of animated life held in stasis.

Roman takes his time to inspect each piece, for even he is not immune to such an awe-inspiring sight. No mere velociraptor, nor even one of the large, docile herbivores. This is the king of the dinosaurs, one which ruled through terror and bloody violence.

"Tyrannosaurus rex," whispers Roman like a hushed benediction, words of power said in homage to a true monarch. His breath frosts in the air and floats away as if his spirit is fleeing this monster. His teeth chatter, and not only from the cold.

The creature is huge, nearly twenty feet tall, yet hunched forward, frozen in mid-stride with jaws agape, as if caught unawares by the calamity which locked it in the ice. The long sweep of its spine is an undulating rollercoaster ride from chunky head to weighty tail. Scales and tough skin cascades across its broad flanks, a non-uniform, dark mossy green, mottled through with distinctive markings of red and brown as if the creature is sculpted from clay and earth.

The legs are thick as tree trunks, making its tiny, stubby forelimbs look hilariously out of place. Each foot has a splay of three large toes, each capped with a claw five inches long. Fat and rounded as an anvil's horn, these aren't made for slashing, but for supporting weight. Yet, if pressed down into flesh they could flatten a ribcage or burst a skull.

Less threatening is the tiny dewclaw at the back of each foot. Like the arms compared to the legs, it forms a strange contrast. Not that the arms are without weapons. Despite the relative smallness of these forelimbs, the claws there are nearly as long as those on the feet. Razor sharp and curved like vicious sickles, they catch the light of the lamp with the same dangerous glint as the massive teeth glimpsed within the gallery of its open jaws.

Scanning these ivory knives is like tapping the keys of a deadly piano, each silent note of terror reverberating in Roman's spine. The teeth are long, longer even than the forelimb claws, and conical like the armour-punching spike of a war-pick yet serrated as a hunting knife designed to saw through flesh and muscle. The line of them leads inevitably to the knotted muscle of its jaw hinge, bulging as if flexing for a bodybuilding show, demonstrating the colossal bite force, five times that of a saltwater crocodile.

And above the jaw, the most dreadful of all features: the single fixed eye. Set deep in a hooded, bony brow on the side of the profiled head, it is as dead as a glassy marble, the eyeball flash frozen, with its lustre dulled by frost. Yet there is a staring intensity which suggests something deeper, something lost which could be rediscovered. There is a subtle glint like a mirrored reflection at its core, but it disappears when the light is moved away.

Roman takes a long breath in and out, and steps back to take the Tyrannosaurus in as a whole. It is a noble creature, a proud monster pausing to have this snapshot taken, a record for future generations of its strength and regal bearing. Yet its quiet poise belies the terrible violence it could unleash in life, and it is easy to imagine the huge jaws closing upon a limb, ripping it off in a gory spray of blood and torn flesh. Roman feels this imaginary pain shoot through him, and he flinches. It takes him a moment to realise the sensation isn't real.

Feeling foolish, he laughs nervously, trying to shake off the fear which spreads through his muscles like a dull ache. But it is hard to let go of when standing in the shadow of the towering dinosaur.

This is no skeleton in a natural history museum. Clothed in flesh, it is a living thing, even if it died long ago.

With a sigh of having to face the inevitable, Roman props his lamp on a rock to shine on the dinosaur and takes up his pickaxe, hefting it above his head. He strikes it into the cave's icy wall, not to free the monster within, but to gain access to it. Hunks of ice come loose and tumble to his feet, but liquid water is also freed in the process. Roman frowns at the gathering pools of water on the floor and the rivulets of the stuff running from somewhere deep in the ice. This is something which has never happened, certainly not in the colder conditions underground, and he looks up warily, wondering if the ceiling of the cave is about to collapse.

Small motes of ice drift downwards like snowflakes and Roman strains to hear any warning sounds. The lump in his throat takes effort to swallow, the gulp sounding loud in his hollow head, but there is no creaking and groaning from the walls to warn of impending cracks and failures in the ice. The only noise is his shallow breathing, and this mists as it passes across the single slash of light from the propped-up lamp.

He lowers the pickaxe, unwilling to risk further heavy strikes. Besides, he is close to the dinosaur's leg now and can begin the final, and more delicate, part of his task. He first readjusts the lamp, focusing its beam on a tighter area. He then takes a small hammer and chisel from his tool bag, chipping away the final layers of ice until he lays bare a tiny section of the dinosaur's scaly hide.

Next, he retrieves his power drill. Its whirring is shockingly loud in this quiet, confined space as he gives it a test, and the shrill whine echoes along the tunnel and back again. It sets his nerves on edge, so he has to take a moment and a few quick breaths. Bracing the drill with both hands, he carefully probes through the armoured scales, judging through experience when he's broken the monster's reptilian skin beneath.

There is no bleeding, not yet, the dinosaur completely frozen. The skin is about a centimetre thick and requires further drilling to penetrate through to the muscle underneath. The drill screams as he pushes deeper into this tough, knotted hide, made tough as plastic by the freezing cold. He has to grit his teeth to stand the torture of it, the vibration jangling up and down his spine like terror, and the sound so sharp it's as if the drill bit is penetrating his skull.

Reaching the inner layers of dense muscle, marbled through with ancient veins, there is a change in the resistance to the drilling, and with it, relief. The bit slides all the way in, and Roman knows he's nearly done.

Retracting the drill, he places it down on the ground and takes out a special syringe. Incorporating a heating element in the syringe itself and attached to a reservoir which can hold a litre of blood, it is a tool designed specifically for this task. He guides it into the hole in the skin he has made and waits for the syringe to warm the tissue within, unlocking the precious dinosaur blood. It flows like thick, red ichor down the tube connecting the syringe to the reservoir and begins to fill it up.

Watching it slide as slowly as his distant thoughts, he daydreams about when he finally harvests enough of the stuff that he'll be set free. But a part of him knows that day will never come. If the reason they need dinosaur blood is so secret—a secret big enough to kill for—then they're never letting him off this accursed continent. He knows too much, little as that is.

His mind wanders around a tangled maze, trying to think of ways to escape, but he keeps coming back to the long dive off the cliff. Which will kill him first, the fall or the freezing water? This question depresses him, and in this moment all he wants is to get out of this bleak cave, full of frozen monsters. It will be enough, for now.

"Come on, come on," he urges the device in his hand. It's taking longer than usual. He rotates the boxy heating element to look at the indicator on the side. The light isn't lit up.

"Fuck, I forgot to turn the thing on."

His finger hovers over a switch, but he hesitates, a doubt scratching at the back of his mind like an insect inside his skull. He glances at the reservoir, half full of congealing blood. He shakes the container and it slops around, leaving red stains up the translucent sides. "If the heating element's not on, then how is the frozen blood flowing at all?"

He looks up at the Tyrannosaurus rex, blinking rapidly in the sparkling cold which tickles his eyeballs. It forms a strobe light optical illusion, one in which he believes he sees the dinosaur move slightly, although surely this is impossible.

"Damn gummies," he says, unsure if he can trust his senses. He shakes his head to reset. Locking in, he forces his eyes to remain open, staring at the dinosaur's leg. His eyes burn, and he wants to blink, but he keeps his vision steady.

There is a throbbing blurring of reality around the peripheries of his sight, the lingering effect of the gummies or his thundering heartbeat, perhaps both, and excitement builds as he thinks he sees something. His eyeballs flex, vision distorted by the quickening pulse in his temple so that he can't be sure. He leans in closer, bracing his gloved hands on the ice either side of the hole he's carved. Through it, he zooms in on a tiny section of the dinosaur and waits.

The agony of dragging time screams at him to blink but he doesn't, needing to know. His sight is a burning laser, narrowing further as he squints, and he wills himself to remain on station.

Then, he sees it.

The movement of the dinosaur, glacially slow, almost imperceptible, is there. A single clawed toe flexes with a tiny flutter of contracting scales.

"Holy shit!" says Roman, flailing his arms and slipping on the ice. He lands on his butt with a pain which jolts up his spine and spikes in his brain. Stars burst behind his eyes, further adding to the sense of movement all around. He blinks these away only for them to be replaced by the sparkles of the ice, glittering like diamonds as his sight dances across the cave wall in awe.

From on the ground the Tyrannosaurus rex seems impossibly large, and terror mixes freely with his awed wonder to produce a heady cocktail of adrenaline and endorphins in Roman's blood.

"Blood," he says, reminded. He scrambles for the dropped syringe device, praying the reservoir hasn't burst. He can't find it at first, so he fetches the lamp, scrambling on hands and knees to frantically search the cave floor. The beam of light plays across the reservoir, the blood dark red and inert as a harvested organ in its translucent bubble, and he breathes a sigh of relief. The syringe is bent, though, and the tube is snapped. Blood oozes from it as if from a severed artery. He quickly kinks it to stop the flow.

"They'd have my head if I didn't get this in," he says, getting to his feet, cradling the blood like a baby. He doesn't know what *they* use it for—research, cloning, some damned immortality elixir—and he doesn't care. Not knowing keeps him alive.

Inside his mind, he sees the penguins diving headfirst, and him joining them, but he dismisses it. For now, he wants to live. He clutches the lamp in one hand, the reservoir of blood in the other, and backs away from the dinosaur slowly, as if any sudden movement will attract its attention, causing it to charge.

The monster remains frozen. Its tiny movements have ceased, such as they were. But living blood flows from the wound in its leg. It mingles with the meltwater which drips down the wall, coming from somewhere up above where it is warmer.

6

Not that it is warm on the surface, at least not to Roman. Even the sun's bright rays provide no relief. Emerging from the cable car at the cave's mouth, the wind slices him like tiny knives, cutting through his thick clothing, stinging his skin and numbing his bones, and he longs to be back in his room. He can't have another gummy—he has too few, and even with the supply ship arriving soon, he can't justify it—but he can be out of the elements, wrapping himself up in the insulating cocoon of the only home he has left.

He forgets that it is in its shelter that he is the most haunted. For now, the wind blows away his thoughts, and he clutches the blood with stiff fingers. It is frozen in the reservoir, a heavy, icy brick which he wants to unburden himself of as soon as possible. The implications of what he's seen in the cave do not follow him into the daylight, dragged away like an exorcised ghost howling words which are lost in the wind.

As he trudges to his snowmobile, bone-tired, there is little to indicate the passage of time while he has been underground. The sun still hangs heavy and low on the horizon, though it has shifted along it, not having arced across the dome of the sky, but instead rotated around the circumference of his tiny world. It is as if Roman lives on the flat face of a clock, the sun's rays the hour hand, and the burning ball of light making a full circle of the horizon's rim each twenty-four hours.

Judging by its position compared to where it was before, he's been underground for sixteen hours; a double shift he'd had no intention of working. Most of that time was lost in transit, wearily yet frantically shuffling through the caves in a confused fugue, goaded by a fear that the Tyrannosaurus had come back to life and was following, hunting him in the darkness. His terror had spiked in waves as his mind played tricks, hearing deafening roars which echoed down tunnels, and sending him the wrong way more than once as his imagination brought to life the shadows created by the crazed swaying of his lamp's beam.

Exhausted, he leans against the snowmobile, his nerves shot from long hours tensed against the possibility of monsters jumping to attack from every hidden angle of the cave. In the sunshine, such fears feel groundless and foolish. He stores the frozen brick of blood under the seat of his vehicle. With it out of his hands, it's easy to think the whole thing a fanciful dream. It wouldn't be the first time his fragile mind had conjured up such a thing, an imaginary piece of excitement born of the desperate boredom inspired by this desolate place. He can't now be sure he saw the claw move.

Looking at the sun, he tries to watch it for long enough to notice its subtle movement as it glides along the horizon. But it's too bright, and he blinks, creating phantasmal replicas of the ball of light upon his retinas. The afterimages dance and move dizzyingly, and for a minute he can't tell which is the real sun and which are the copies created by a trick of his senses.

"The Tyrannosaurus didn't move," Roman tells himself with false certainty as he climbs astride the snowmobile.

He squeezes his eyes shut and waits for the circles of light to settle into a single glowing ball. When he opens his eyes, the sun is no longer moving, or at least its movement isn't perceptible in the moment he glances its way. Unable to take his bearings from such an unreliable point of reference, he instead looks at the GPS on the dashboard of his snowmobile, having faith that it will take him in the right direction.

***

Revving across the icy field of velociraptors, Roman steers towards walking figures, black silhouettes against the infinite white. He skids to a halt before a pair of them and leaves the engine idling, burbling away. Lifting his goggles, he nevertheless attempts to keep his feelings hidden behind a familiar mask of social propriety.

"Alright," he says in way of greeting.

"Roman," says one of the figures, peeling off his ski mask to reveal a face covered with a second insulating layer of fuzzy grey beard.

"Trent," says Roman with a nod and a weary smile. He's less pleased when the other man turns to face him. Roman should have recognised him by his vast bulk.

"Brock," says Roman, regretting stopping. "What are you doing here?"

Brock unravels a scarf from across his mouth. "Working, like you should be doing."

"I'm only just coming in off the last shift."

Trent raises his bushy eyebrows. Roman grins feebly and shrugs by tucking his head down into his shoulders protectively. He feels his social mask slipping but not so much he's willing to tell the whole truth.

"I got a bit lost," he says, another little piece of it working its way out of his lips before he can squeeze them shut. His eyes dart furtively between the two men, gauging their response. Brock scrunches up his face.

"You must be tired," says Trent. He lays a hand on Roman's shoulder. Roman lets the touch thaw him out a bit, and he raises his head out of his shell.

"Fuck tired, he's a load behind," interjects Brock, slashing his arm down through the air as if trying to cut the invisible sympathetic tie between the two others. Roman slumps down as if it were the only thing keeping him up. He knows there will be consequences for this. His body suddenly feels very heavy and he looks at the base longingly.

"We'll catch him up," Trent says to Brock.

"We've got our own quota to fill," answers Brock, munching angrily on meaty lips, his words a mumbled grumble.

"You must be cold and hungry," Trent says, turning back to Roman.

Roman doesn't look at Brock, the man's eyes burrowing into him, and he nods with a hanging head, finally letting the events of the day overtake him.

"Head into the cafeteria and grab a hot drink and some food, take it up to your room and rest," says Trent.

Roman's head shoots up, his eyes pleading. "I've got to log this blood. I'm already behind on my quota."

"We'll log it in your name," says Trent, nudging Roman to lift his butt so that he can retrieve the blood from the storage compartment.

"The hell we can!" says Brock, shoving Roman down so that the compartment snaps shut like the jaws of a beast.

Trent pulls his fingers back reflexively, giving Brock a hard glare. "We're working right by the base today."

"So? That's our good luck."

"And this is Antarctica. We're in this mess together, remember?"

Roman knows he means their captivity as much as the harsh continent. No one ever refers to it directly, even though it's the dominating factor of all their lives. He glances down at the velociraptors beneath their feet, trapped in the ice, and feels not so much different to them.

"We fill our quotas, we get out of here," says Brock, repeating the well-worn lie they tell themselves and each other.

"Sure we do," says Trent. "*All* of us. Together."

There's an edge to the way Trent says this which Roman feels is infused with a deeper meaning, but he's too distracted by the velociraptors, which seem closer to the surface than they did before. And the ice is a bit slushy as he skates his cleats across it. He turns his gaze to the horizon, where the omnipresent sun seems to glow a little fiercer today. Its sunlight bounces powerfully off the mirror of the ice plain, dazzling him with its brilliance. He squirms and squints.

"What's the matter with you?" asks Brock, turning to loom over him. He blocks out the low sun with his bulk, casting a long shadow which seems to quiver in the frigid wind.

"What? Nothing," says Roman, blinking myopically like a mole up at the dark shape of the man. Brock's face is a featureless mass, terrifyingly inhuman, his mouth a black hole in a black plain, seeming to swallow the infinitely bright light of the tundra.

"You're high," accuses Brock, the fat, shadowy head leaning in to scrutinise Roman's eyes. Roman blinks dumbly, the only response he can muster to the accusation, aware words will betray him, even though the gummies have long since abandoned him to the harsh corners of undiluted reality, and anything he says will only betray him as weird and different, like always, and nothing more. But it's enough to be condemned.

Brock turns to Trent. "That's why he got *lost*." He emphasises the word with finger quotations, and then kicks a leg, as if punting Roman's useless ass out into the wilderness. "He's out there getting high in the tunnels."

Roman wishes this to be true. Or still true, at least. Now he's just swooning with exhaustion and dizzy with the blinding light of the ice field.

"You got anything to drink?" he asks, his throat dry so that the words come out as a strangled croak.

"That's contraband," says Brock in such a way as to deflect attention away from any of his own after-hours relaxation activities.

"He means water," says Trent, retrieving an insulated bottle and handing it over. Roman gulps the liquid greedily despite its coldness. He wipes the excess from his lips before it freezes there and hands back the bottle.

Trent takes a gulp himself, smacking his lips with relish. "Wish we had some vodka, though," he says, side-eyeing Brock, who shakes his head almost imperceptibly.

Roman doesn't care either way. He doesn't drink. But he desperately wants—*needs*—another gummy. He mentally counts the days remaining until the supply ship. Maybe he can make his stash stretch. Or he can say fuck it, take what he needs now, and leave the suffering for later. He's suffering now, anyway, his whole body and mind a riot of exhaustion and pain, and so he lifts his butt, letting Trent retrieve the brick of frozen blood.

"Tyrannosaurus," says Roman, not sure he should trust such a vital load to anyone. But Trent gives him a reassuring wink. He hands the brick to Brock.

"Run that in and log it," he says.

"But—" Brock begins.

"Did I fucking stutter?" snaps Trent, the violent edge to his voice a sharp slap which boxes Brock across the ears, making the big man wince.

Brock scowls as he takes the blood, shooting a look at Roman which speaks of simmering violence. Roman is too tired to care. The big man stomps off towards the base.

"I'll change the roster so your next load is velociraptor," says Trent, stamping the ground with a splash of melted water. Unlike the tyrannosaurus, the velociraptors there do not stir, for which Roman is thankful for. He's so tired he's ready to believe he imagined the whole thing.

Trent brandishes a metal tube, shakes it in the air like it's a sword and he's a leader rallying his troops with a rousing speech. But he doesn't say any words, restrained by a discretion which Roman sees as a playful twinkle in the older man's eyes. Gripping it two handed like a stake he's about to drive into the heart of a vampire, he drives the tube down into the ice, cracking through to the dinosaur, which is buried only skin deep. Leaning his whole weight on it he pushes the device into the velociraptor's body to begin the process of extracting the creature's valuable lifeblood.

7

Roman is completely drained. Entering his room, he closes the door behind him, places a steaming tray of a roast dinner and a mug of hot chocolate on his desk, and stands in front of the mirror. His face is pale as snow, with a blue tinge like the ice fields. It is as if his flesh itself has become one with the desolate landscape outside. His mouth is pinched with cold, and the lines in his brow speak of residual fear settling in as perpetual worry. He can't forget what happened, the way the Tyrannosaurus moved, even if he thinks it an illusion caused by the gummies.

Gummies… He goes to the drawer of the desk, ignoring the succour of the hot food and drink on the tray, not trusting the relief it offers and going for the easy option instead. He needs it, and he doesn't think twice—not about the supply ship, and certainly not about the other precious commodity he has hidden in his wall—as he downs one of the gummies after only a few rabid chews.

He takes a few deep breaths, impatient for the drug to settle into his stomach and infuse him with the warmth he so desperately craves. He sits at his desk and eats, the food more a distraction than a nourishing force; it merely crowds the gummy in his guts and makes it take longer to kick in. But he's hungry, despite what his brain tells him, and his stomach growls like a ravenous monster, sounding how he imagines the dinosaur in the ice would sound if it were to get free.

Free? It isn't possible. It is dead, like Roman, trapped in the substrate of Antarctica, both of them *one* with it. But Roman feels his body heating up, warmed by the room and food, melting the frosty crust which clings to his clothing like rime. It sloughs off him like a second skin, soaking into the carpet, making a wet patch which he stares at. He sees shapes in it like those seen in clouds, his brain interpreting them—people running before a monster—but quickly forgetting as the stain spreads, changing shapes until he gets a glimpse of the outline of a ragged continent, one he's seen all too often on maps. Antarctica.

Steam rises from the stain, and it shrinks over a long time as he stares, its coastline morphing and collapsing, and it is only after it completely disappears that Roman realises that the gummy has kicked in, warping time, keeping him comfortably fixated, and now he is too hot in his heavy clothing.

He stands, feeling claustrophobic in the padded jackets and pants, the heavy jumpers and thick insulated socks. He fights his way free, suffocating in the heat after so long being cold. It is unpleasant and he groans and moans wordlessly, limbs tortured as he struggles to free them of their constricting bindings.

Soon, after much effort, like pulling himself out of a womb, he is naked and able to move again. He looks around his room, a tiny cave he doesn't know how to get out of, and he stomps around its tiny confines, frustrated and angry to find himself locked away after only so recently becoming free.

***

"It's locked," he says, many hours later, with the gummy's effect subsiding.

He'd spent a good portion of that time pretending he was a dinosaur on a rampage, gaining no small pleasure from imagining biting the likes of Brock in half. His blood had washed hot across his teeth and flowed down his throat, filling him with invigorating warmth. It had made him happy and content. Drowsiness had overwhelmed him and he'd passed out on the bed, the cooling hot chocolate left unfinished, curdling on his desk.

Now, with his wits returned, and with them the anxiety, he has gotten dressed and, with dextrous human hands rather than the clumsy, clawed arms of a Tyrannosaurus, he has gone to the door of his room, turning the handle to exit.

Only he can't.

He rattles the handle frantically. His first response is to take another gummy to calm down. He dashes to his desk, but he knows what he'll find before he even gets to the drawer and opens the bag. He tips it upside down. Nothing falls out. They are all gone, he's eaten them all—tiny morsels gulped down in his ravenous hallucinatory rampage—and he is locked in sobriety as sure as he's locked in the room.

"Help," he bleats. But who will hear him? Who will help him when he can't even help himself? Panic spikes in his brain as he realises he's a vulnerable, squishy human, with more in common with the gummies than the dinosaur he had imagined himself to be in his drug-fuelled fugue. He is prey in a world of monsters.

Searching frantically for a means to escape this daunting reality, he goes to the window and draws back the blackout curtains. Brilliant white light shines in, and he hisses as if it burns the exposed skin of his face. His eyes sting as he peers through the glass at the blinding landscape, and for a moment he can't make out any details, everything a uniform brightness. But soon, little pieces of it start to snap off to form fragments of shadows, and with them comes depths and the outline of things.

He sees black silhouettes in the distance he takes to be people. They gather into huddled bunches, heads on pivots, looking about in panic. They run together as one, fleeing fat black lines which scar the landscape, an expanding spider web of crevices opening beneath their feet. One of these, much larger than the rest, carves up the tundra with an audible cracking sound. The crazed zigzag of splitting ice shoots off towards the nearby coast. It cuts the pack of figures in two and they scatter individually, only to come together again as two frightened masses rather than one. They cease running, instead bouncing on the spot, their heads bobbing up and down in distress.

Roman frowns and leans forward to see better, shielding his eyes with his hand to cut the glare.

"They're penguins," he says, the silhouettes coming into focus.

The ice they stand on fractures further, the whole coastline a maze of cracks. The cracks are black chasms, growing wider as he watches, as if the continent itself is falling to bits. Penguins lose their footing as the pieces of ice they perch upon tilt at alarming angles, and they tumble into the black pits. Roman feels his heart gripped in a vice and he slaps the glass with his hand, impotent to help. None of the penguins emerge again, their fate unknown, and Roman can only speculate whether they escape into the water below the ice or are crushed between the massive grinding masses of shifting ice.

This scene repeats as far as he can see to the left and right, the whole coastline a shattered ruin of crumbling ice falling into the ocean and floating away. It is like a huge flotilla of white ships setting sail. And in amongst them there is a single red one, standing out in violent contrast like blood on the snow. It is an actual ship, one Roman recognises.

"The resupply," he says in hushed reverence, his breath fogging up the glass.

8

"It's here early," says Roman in alarm, a hot flush burning up his face and neck. He loosens his collar with one hand. With the other, he wipes the condensation of his breath from the window to confirm that he really saw what he saw, that is not another gummy-induced hallucination.

The ship is still there, a huge, red-hulled ice breaker with a rising tower of white on its deck like a floating skyscraper dotted with windows.

"I need to get out there," he says, running to the door. His mind is myopically focused on reaching the ship and his black market contact, so that he's turning the handle before its resistance and dull clicking reminds him it is locked.

"Fuck!"

He stomps his foot in frustration, and his socked foot slips on something, a piece of the ground coming loose, white like the ice flows outside. It's paper thin. It *is* paper, sliding under his foot with a soft whisper against the carpeted floor.

Roman bends down, picks it up, frowning at the writing there. He blinks his brightness-blinded eyes, trying to get the black printed writing to stop flashing negative like an afterimage. He recognises the letterhead first, a silhouette like a cluster of hieroglyphs he has learned to fear. It projects off the page like a hologram as he blinks, imprinting itself directly onto his retinas and burning into his brain like a brand. It is the symbol of his forced servitude. Below a familiar logo—an outline of Antarctica with a drop of blood superimposed—is an even more familiar set of letters, the stamp of authority for all official communications.

"Tottenham," Roman says, not reading the name there, but knowing all the same what it says. This is not the name of the organisation, which has only the logo to identify its shadowy existence, but that of a man, although the two are synonymous.

Roman's sight calms down, though not his heart, which beats faster as he reads on. It is a memo from the base commandant—an ephemeral figure unseen yet constantly present in the form of directives such as these—slipped under his door to inform Roman he is confined to quarters. The reason: unlogged quotas.

"Missing blood?" Roman says, although he shouldn't be surprised. He turns automatically to glance in the direction of his secret hiding place. But as he reads on, he sees the quantity is wrong, and it hits him like a wave.

"Brock didn't log the Tyrannosaurus blood in my name!" he says, hurling the piece of paper away from him. It flutters and floats in the air, defying the force of his anger as it drifts slowly to the floor. "He logged it himself to get the shift off."

Roman takes two quick steps to the wall of his room. "Or he's as dumb as I am," he says, his anger directed at himself now. He grips the giant penguin poster covering the wall and rips it down. Behind it, the wall looks uniform, unblemished except for the tack marks where he'd stuck up the poster. His hand glides across its smooth surface. Invisible to the eye, yet felt by his searching fingertips, are slight lines.

"How did he find out?" Roman says, fuming at himself. Like a secret ritual, he performs the precise set of movements to pop the panel loose from the wall, revealing the treasure hidden behind. An inert, dark crimson mass, it comes to life as he pulls it out, glistening like a fat ruby in the fluorescent light as he turns it in his hands. The blood in the container sloshes thickly, an echo of his sludgy heartbeat, straining in his veins.

"I've got it," he says like a loser gambler, begging the loan shark for more time to pay. He knows the commandant can't hear, and even if he could, the blood in his hands is only half of what he owes. And he has other debts.

He rushes to the window, holding the blood up like a heart cut from a sacrificial victim on an altar. He shows it to the ship in desperation as the vessel's bulk eclipses the sun's rays for an agonising instant. The darkness of winter clouds Roman's brain for a second, and he despairs. He's cut off. His contact—with its supply of black market gummies—is on that ship, but he can't reach them to trade this blood for that which sustains his existence. Without the soothing drug, there is no momentary release from the prison of being, no small death to take refuge in, staving off the more permanent solution which crowds his sober thoughts.

His heart sinks as he pictures himself diving into the cold water, and there being an even deeper darkness waiting, far below, to swallow him whole, the world forgetting he ever existed.

But then the sun comes out again, the ship churning on to reveal its burning orb. With its red paint, sparkling with reflected light, the vessel looks like the still-beating heart of the sea, cut loose but attempting to drive itself back into the body of the continent. It rams the shifting mass of ice flows with its breaker bow. The torturous shrieks of metal on ice grate at Roman's nerves.

"You can have it, just let me out," he pleads through gritted teeth, wanting the pain to stop, the agony of his existence, trapped in an empty head, in an empty room, on an empty continent. It's no life, only a barren wasteland with no hope, and he wants out, wants to actually live his life and be free. But he isn't free. The desire for the gummies is strong, mini-withdrawals bringing out the goosebumps on his skin. Sweat pools at the base of his spine, sending a shiver up the vertebrae. It strikes his skull like a cold bullet and ricochets around his hollow skull, obliterating rational thought.

"I said take it!" he screams, shaking the viscous blood. It feels hot in his hands, and he wants to be rid of it. But he knows this is impossible. The ship, driving into the fractured coast in its attempt to deliver its much-needed cargo of supplies and pick up the even more precious load of blood, cannot dock. With a huge eruption of tossed up water, the harbour it is aiming for falls into the sea, carried away by an avalanche of collapsing ice cliffs, their structure weakened as if by the melting rays of a sun grown too hot.

It is a humbling sight, mankind's hubris in attempting to tame this wild continent laid bare. He watches as more of the cliffs slide away, crushing black shapes. It is with a sense of detachment that Roman realises these are not penguins, but men. He feels no relief to have been kept here against his will instead of lurking about the docks, trying to trade his ill-gotten blood for drugs. A part of him wishes he was there, even if it means losing his life, because he can't picture a life without the gummies to take the edge off.

Now he must face the harsh truth of reality. And it is the same reality which everyone on the base must face. The resupply ship, seeing it cannot reach a safe harbour on the coast to unload, is turning away, fleeing from the cataclysmic chaos of the collapsing ice cliffs. With it goes a year's worth of food, clothes, medicine, machine parts, batteries, and all the supplies required to sustain life in this hellhole.

"But you *need* us," says Roman in wheedling, whining desperation, pressing the container of blood up against the window. As he watches the ship, though, he realises this isn't true.

Knocked loose by the crumbling coast, there are irregular icy shapes floating in the water. They look like giant, uncut gemstones, and are just as precious. They sparkle in the sunlight like beacons, attracting his attention, but also that of the ship, which turns towards them, keen to recover this invaluable prize. A huge crane on the vessel's deck hauls each of these miniature icebergs from the water in turn, giving Roman a clear view of what is contained in the icy blocks: frozen dinosaurs, and with them, their blood.

"Stegosaurus, triceratops, ankylosaurus, parasaurolophus," says Roman, listing those he sees plucked from the ocean. "But no Tyrannosaurus. You still don't have the most prized one. *I* have it here, in my hands. You'll be back."

It is some small consolation, the only thing which calms Roman down. But the ship, after hours of scooping the scattered diamonds of ice, shows no sign it cares as it turns its stern on the base and heads back towards the distant horizon, taking Roman's whole world with it.

He clutches the pint of Tyrannosaurus blood, the only thing he has left, as he slides to the floor, crinkling his penguin poster. He slides his hand across it to smooth its creases but can't undo what's been done. It will never hold the same shape again.

A piece of it comes away, though it doesn't tear. His fingers grip this rectangle, crumpling it in clawed fingers. It is the memo from the commandant. He can't bring himself to read it again, but he doesn't have to. He remembers every damning word, and a part of him welcomes this punishment, knowing he deserves it. Not that his situation is any worse than anyone else on the base now. Starvation is coming.

He looks at the blood. It sloshes like tomato soup, rich and vital, if not appetizing or inviting. He frowns and shakes his head. He's not that desperate, though a time might come when he is, especially if he remains locked in this room. Sullen, he looks at the piece of paper in his other hand, and the furrows on his brow deepen. There is something written on the back in black biro.

He puts the blood down and flattens the crumpled piece of paper on the floor.

“Best if you stay here. Signed, T,” reads Roman. That’s it. He turns the paper over to see if there’s any more writing he’s missed. There isn’t.

“What the hell kind of sick joke is this? Of course I’m staying here. I’m locked in. Who wrote this?”

His first thought is T for Tottenham, but this makes no sense. He curls his lips and shakes his head. No, it’s the only other T he knows.

“Trent,” he says, sure of it, although this only confuses him further, not knowing why the man would send such a message. And why on the back of an official memo, of all things?

As if in answer to his question, gunfire erupts outside his window.

9

Roman grips the container of blood in reflexive terror, his heart being squeezed in his chest by the same surge of shock and adrenaline. It brings him to his feet with a jolt, skin tingling as if he's being electrocuted. He dances from foot to foot, looking left and right, not knowing what to do and where to go as he hears more gunshots from beyond the building.

The popping of small arms fire is interspersed with the sustained rattle of automatic weapons, like a swarm of angry insects buzzing around, bursting balloons with their stingers. Both are drowned out by a larger boom which boxes Roman around the ears with a hard slap of sound. His knees go weak and he stumbles, almost dropping the blood. He clutches it tightly like it's his heart worn outside his chest; if it breaks, he dies. It's all he has left to barter with. All his life is worth.

He feels pathetically vulnerable, as fragile as the plastic holding the blood in, and wants to take shelter, from the chaos of sound as much as from the violence. But even if the steel walls of the base are thick enough to stop bullets, they cannot block the sound, and it continues to shake him, the confusion of the unknown painful.

"What the fuck is going on?" he shouts above the din of another explosion. He feels the magnetic pull of the window, his curiosity dragging him where courage cannot. He drops to his knees and scrambles over to it, peering over the sill.

The first thing he sees is fire. It is a strange sight against the white of the ice and snow, the flames almost invisible, merely distorting what they burn in a shimmering heat haze. But the smoke is dark, rising in curling plumes from a gutted building a hundred metres from the central base. It's the guardhouse, where soldiers shelter from the elements between their patrols to keep those outside out and those inside in.

Now they, too, burn, running around like lit beacons as if attempting to warn others of danger, or else laying still, smouldering face down in the snow. The screams of the former are nearly as chilling as the silence of the latter, and Roman ducks his head back down as more gunfire spanks off the steel plating of the base in a shower of sparks.

"Who's shooting? Who's shooting?" he asks, over and over. The soldiers, his mind tells him. It is an incomplete and infuriating answer. Who are they fighting? Has someone finally come to rescue him and the others? No, not likely, because who knows they are here?

Perhaps some other country or organisation has come to claim the dinosaurs and their blood? More probable, but the forces which surround this region of Antarctica have resisted every probe. Time and again, Roman has seen a ship or a plane approach, only to witness their violent deaths, the inevitability of their demise robbing him of any hope of escape.

So, who has been able to get this close?

Unable to stand the uncertainty, Roman lifts his head to peer out the window again. There are spatters of blood on the snow outside his window, and a string of reddened footprints which lead to a body. Face down, he can't see who they are, but they're wearing not a soldier's uniform, but regular cold weather clothes, much like Roman's.

His breathing becomes ragged, fearing a massacre, with himself a victim. With a flash of violent realisation, picturing himself in their place, he finds he wants to live, and the vision of diving off the cliff with the penguins which has haunted him for weeks vanishes like mist. Instead, another spectre of doom, external to himself, takes its place as a large man holding a machine gun appears by the dead body. They bend over, rummaging under the collar for a pulse, and then straighten with a shake of their head. The weapon held level at the hip, the barrel tracks with the man's eyes as they scan for threats in a three-sixty-degree motion.

Roman's breath catches in his throat as their face comes into view.

It's Brock.

***

Their eyes lock for the briefest of moments. Roman tells his body to move. Time hangs suspended as Roman begins to duck back down, but not before he sees Brock open his mouth to shout, waving an arm to beckon others and pointing with the barrel of his gun. Dropping below the sill, Roman hears the shout, its urgent essence if not the actual words, and he's aware of what it means.

He's fucked.

But he can do nothing; he hasn't forgotten the door is locked, not this time. He's a distressed rat in a tiny cage, though this doesn't stop him from scrabbling at the walls, the window, the door, in a frantic attempt at escape.

Gunfire inside the building now, growing closer with each shot, louder in his ears, each one feeling like it's aimed at his head. The execution is coming. He sees his inert body, face down in the icy slush of the tundra, blood leaking out to stain the ground like some macabre snow cone.

But that's not how it will happen. He will die here, in this small room, as he always dreaded, even as he dreamed of something greater, of escape just before the end, a chance to live, even if it meant death anyway; an adventure, full of excitement, and yes, danger, he could risk danger as long as it led away from this slow, agonising grind into an icy grave at the edge of the world.

It's coming too quickly though, the excitement too much of a spike, leading not to a thrill to make life worth living, only blind panic in the rush to the finish line. He'll bounce between the walls of this room for a few moments more, overtaken by terror, and then the door will open. A small movement, just a finger on a trigger, followed by short, sharp sound, and a bullet will ricochet around the inside of his skull, rattling like dice in a cup, destroying all his bad thoughts, but all the good ones too.

He wants more from existence than this. But who is he to ask for it?

The gunshots cease, and there is a tense anticipation like an infinite void. The silence becomes agonising and Roman's fear spikes, driving all thoughts from his mind as the terror reaches fever pitch. Basic survival instincts find no outlet, fight or flight both useless. He can only quake, the blood in his hands sloshing with the tremors.

Footsteps in the hall are like the soft ticking of a clock. He has these few seconds to live, but he can put them to no use.

"Get it over with!" he shouts, his nerves snapping with the strain. The footsteps cease. A pause. Roman watches in fevered dread as the doorknob twists, his palms slick with sweat as he rubs them together fretfully. A click of release. The door opens inward with a sick creak.

Brock stands in the doorway, a dumb, violent grin upon his broad face. He fills the space with his bulk, barring the way. There is a spattering of blood on his jacket, a drop of it on his chin. As if feeling Roman's eyes upon it, Brock lifts his gloved hand, wipes at the drop, only succeeding in smearing it across his skin like war paint. He holds his glove out to look at the blood staining its fabric, his smile broadening. His eyes rise to meet Roman's again as his hand drops to the automatic weapon slung across his front.

"Alright," says Brock.

10

"Stop that," says Trent, shouldering Brock aside to enter the room. "You're scaring him to death."

Brock's grin sours but he lets the other man past. "He's not with us," he says to Trent's back.

Trent doesn't turn. He crouches before Roman, who looks at him with the awe reserved for a delivering angel. Trent extends a hand, which Roman goes to take, expecting to be helped up. But he's still holding the container of dinosaur blood, and Trent takes this instead of his hand.

Standing, Trent looks it over like a pawn store owner appraising an item of its worth. He sucks his teeth thoughtfully and looks at Roman, still on the floor. "Tyrannosaurus?" he asks, speculatively. Roman dumbly nods his head.

"Good, good," says Trent. "See, Brock, he's one of us. Or, at least, he's not one of *them*." He jerks his head at the window in the general direction of the burning guardhouse. With a placid, benign look on his face, he takes in Roman's room. With an appreciative whistle, he goes to the hiding place in the wall, the removed panel on the bed below it. "Very clever, hiding this away. I knew you were up to something."

"Doesn't mean he can be trusted," snarls Brock. His eyes are fixed on Roman, the muzzle of his weapon a third eye, sensing deceit. Roman recoils, afraid it sees his intentions, whatever they are. He doesn't know himself, wanting only to live out the next few minutes.

"Take it easy, Brock," says Trent. He turns to Roman. "We're not going to kill you, are we?" he says, the first part a statement, the second a question, as if the answer depends upon Roman rather than these two killers. Roman notices the pistol holstered at Trent's hip as he steps close, hanging over his head like Damocles sword. Roman's nerves are a taut string, set to snap at any moment.

He shakes his head, the movement not stopping at his neck. It travels through his whole body, a shiver of fear, motivating him to be compliant.

"Good, good," says Trent. He tosses the Tyrannosaurus blood from hand to hand casually as if it were a baseball. "Because we need more of this if we're going to have any leverage. And you know where we can find it."

***

Roman stumbles down the hall after Trent and Brock, his limbs weak. He doesn't want to go with them, but it's better than staying in the room, and already he feels an invisible tie between them and him. Like it or not, he's a part of their rebellion, too, if only for the fact that he's still alive. And that's not certain to last, either. If he isn't useful, or worse, actively obstructs them, then he'll be the one face down in the snow, his lifeblood leaking out.

"Please, can I have something to eat?" he says, his stomach growling.

"That's right," says Trent with a snap of his fingers. "You've been locked up for three days."

"Three days?" Roman's head spins like a gyroscope, a sort of time-related vertigo overcoming him. Gorging on his supply of gummies, he had stepped out of time. Re-entering its stream at the rate of everyone else is dislocating, and he instinctually peers around for a clock, a calendar, something to anchor him solidly, not trusting mere words, especially not those of Trent.

"I'm surprised he didn't drink the damn blood, then," says Brock. The smear of blood is still on his chin, and his fat, pink tongue probes for its stickiness absentmindedly.

"Drink it?" says Roman, trying to sound incredulous, as if it hadn't occurred to him, the idea itself monstrous.

"He'd have drunk half a million dollars' worth," says Trent, hefting the pint of blood in his hand like he's weighing up an ingot of gold.

"Half a million…" Roman's incredulity is real this time. "No wonder I got that deckhand on the supply ship to agree to a trade of a few bags of edibles."

"Is that why you were hiding it?" scoffs Brock. "I wonder if it's the same guy we use," he says to Trent.

"Not likely," says Trent. "Totally different kettle of fish, a few bags of contraband versus what we were asking for."

"The guns," says Roman.

Trent turns around and makes a *click, clack, bang* sound, pretending to shoot Roman with his finger and thumb as a pistol. "You got it," he says with a wink. A grin dances at the corner of his lips.

"Good thing he didn't figure it out earlier," grumbles Brock. "Guy's so smart he's dumb. He would have shot his mouth off to the wrong person and blown the whole thing."

"Lucky he's got no friends, or I would've had to shoot him," says Trent, his grin turning wolfish. He pushes open double doors, and as they enter the cafeteria, the truth of Trent's threat is made apparent.

The room is full of people, all of them civvies. Half of them are dead. Their bodies lay where they were gunned down mid-meal. The other half sit alongside the slumped corpses, some laughing and joking, others grim and sullen, all of them with plates of food taken from the buffet. Steam rises from the hot food as well as from the freshly slain, mingled into a fog of condensation by the cycling air vents in the ceiling. It creates a sticky sweet tang in the air which cloys in the back of Roman's throat and makes him gag even as his stomach rumbles.

"You still got to eat," says Brock, slapping Roman on the back to shove him forward, as if this is some type of loyalty test. If it is, Roman knows he'll pass with flying colours. His stomach is queasy at the sight of the dead, but empty enough not to care. He feels faint with the lack of food and the foetid stench, so he all too happily rushes to fill several plates on a tray. Holding it close to his nose to ward off the smell of blood and spilt guts, he walks to a table to sit by himself, as he's always done.

"No, no," says Brock, locking fingers like the grip of a vice on his shoulder. Roman winches and hunches down, but he can't duck out of the hold Brock has on him. He's steered around to sit at a table, not by himself, but with Brock, as well as with Trent and several corpses. The dead are arranged either side of Trent, locked in poses so that the scene resembles the painting of Jesus at the last supper.

"Just so we know what side you're on," says Brock with a single bark of laughter. "You're either with us." He waves a butter knife around vaguely at the living. Then he uses it to prod a corpse. "Or you're with them."

"I want to live," Roman says simply, hoping this is enough, though his face betrays his unease as Brock uses the same knife to butter a hunk of bread.

"Good," says Trent. "We've got a lot of work to do securing the base. But the blood is still a priority. It's what this is all about."

"Not about gaining our freedom?" asks Roman.

"Who said anything about *you* being free?" says Brock, jabbing the butter knife into Roman's side and giving it a twist.

Roman winces. "I just thought—"

"Best leave the thinking to me," says Trent. "But no, we're not breaking out of here. Not yet at least. We're just taking over the operation. You heard what a pint of this good blood goes for on the black market. We harvest our fill and we go back to the world as rich men."

Roman thinks this is madness, that the authorities will never let them leave this continent, not with millions of dollars of dinosaur blood, and certainly not with the secret of this place to tell the world. But a man's dead body slumps against Roman's shoulder, and this reminds him of his peril, so he keeps his mouth shut.

"Aww, look who finally made a friend," says Brock.

Roman goes to shove the corpse away, but Brock leans over him.

"Now, now, no need to be shy," he says, draping the cadaver's lifeless arm over Roman's shoulder. "Ah, young love."

Roman stares into his food, wilfully letting the steam fog up his eyeballs, not wanting to be here. This is not his revolution. He's traded one set of sadistic jailors for another.

"Stop fucking about," snaps Trent with a clatter of cutlery on his empty plate. "We've got work to do."

"But I'm still eating," protests Brock.

"Time is money."

Roman doesn't waste that precious time complaining, ramming as much food into his mouth as he can before Brock hauls him to his feet.

"Get your hands off me," says Roman, shucking out of the grip. Brock raises an eyebrow and glances at Trent. Trent shakes his head subtly and jerks it towards the exit.

The two men lead the way. Roman follows them to the door of his own volition, but his feet are leaden, his movements stiff, as if he's already dead, he just doesn't know it yet.

11

Outside, the sun is a blinding orb which saturates the landscape with light. The snow is a field of scintillating diamonds, promising riches to any willing to reach down with their hands and scoop them up. But Roman knows there are things buried in that snow, things that are best left undisturbed. Trent and Brock have other ideas.

"Let's go get some blood," says Brock. And there is plenty of that in the snow too, human as well as dinosaur, one flowing more freely than the other today.

In response to Brock's boyish enthusiasm, Trent grunts, distracted as he waves over some men carrying rifles. He disperses them with terse words and sharp gestures of his hands. The men move off to their tasks, securing what supplies remain, enough for now, Roman is sure, but with the ship turned away, how long before they are starved out?

He looks to the coast. It is a fractured wasteland, the reflective ice riven with cracks like a massive pane of shattered glass. Colossally huge chunks of ice, their sides steep as cliffs, float free, crashing into each other, further disintegrating into smaller fragments as if breeding and multiplying. The destruction reaches nearly to the base, which looks to be in danger of falling into the sea.

"Damn global warming," says Trent, scratching his bearded chin as he takes in the same sight as Roman.

"Not your work then?" asks Roman, genuinely surprised. He thought it too much of a coincidence to be anything but part of the plan, the timing of the attack aligned with this destruction. He had assumed the same explosives which had done for the guardhouse had split the ice, preventing reinforcements from the supply ship coming ashore.

"You think this," says Trent, indicating the cataclysmic alteration of the landscape with a sweep of his hand, "is within my power?"

"It would be a godlike feat," admits Roman.

Trent shades his eyes with the same hand, looking up at the sun. "Godlike indeed."

Roman doesn't look, not wanting to be blinded, but he can feel the heat of the sun's rays bearing down on him like a physical weight. Beneath his booted feet, the ice is a melted slurry which splashes as he kicks his way towards the snowmobiles Brock has brought around for them to ride. He sits astride one of them, the engine idling.

"You're up front," says Trent, nodding to the other. Roman sits himself down, flexes his hands on the handlebars, surprised to be in control of something, anything.

"Don't get any ideas," says Trent, sitting behind him. He pokes something into Roman's kidney. Whether it's a finger or the barrel of a pistol, Roman doesn't know.

"You want me to start us up?" Roman asks, playing cautious.

"Don't be a smartarse," Trent growls in his ear. His words rumble through Roman's torso and spread through the vehicle below as Trent leans over and hits the electric starter. His hand indeed holds a pistol, and Roman has the mad idea of grabbing it. But before he can decide whether this is a good idea, or even possible, the pistol slides back into place in the small of his back, his chance of escape with it.

"Take us to the money," shouts Brock over the rev of his engine as he gives the throttle a slight twist. Roman grinds his teeth, not liking to be told what to do by the likes of Brock, and does the same. The two snowmobiles snarl antagonistically at each other like a pair of beasts squaring off for a fight.

"Lead the way, then," says Trent, and his words carry more authority, coming as they do from the barrel of a gun. Goaded by the threat jabbing him in the back, Roman twists the throttle and turns out towards the tundra in a skidding move which throws a spray of snow into Brock's face.

Trent laughs with genuine mirth, the sound bubbling in Roman's ear like releasing pressure. The pressure of the pistol in his back eases off as well, and Roman gives the snowmobile a push, icy wind blowing past him, with nothing in front but open tundra and the distant mountains. For the moment, he can believe he's free. As long as he ignores the weight at his back.

***

"Where the fuck did these rocks come from?" says Trent, his voice rattling with vibration as the snowmobile jolts across the rugged terrain. Roman slows, trying to dodge the black lumps jutting from the icy ground, but they're everywhere, and he succeeds only in hitting each all the harder for having slowed. The snowmobile jars them as they jostle their way over one after another.

"Yeah, I don't remember the tundra having speed bumps," jokes Roman, but Trent doesn't laugh this time, his fickle humour flipping like a coin to show its other face. The gun returns to Roman's back, but it has little effect, because there's nothing Roman can do. He considers taking off at high speed, perhaps coasting over the top of the dark mounds, but he'd more likely hit one at the wrong angle with the snowmobile's skis, sending them flying. A crash would be certain, but perhaps this isn't such a bad idea; a roll of the dice that Trent would be hurt and not Roman.

But Brock is following close behind with his automatic rifle, and Roman wouldn't get far on foot before he got a bullet in the back. And besides, where would he go? Not back to the base, where Trent's supporters would string him up. He looks to the mountains. They look uninviting, like sharp, stone knives from prehistoric times. They stand sentinel, guarding the way, but there is a narrow pass between two of the peaks. Normally it is packed with snow year-round, even in the summer, but this has melted like the coastal ice to form a river at the base of the mountains. It snakes its way across the landscape like a road to freedom. But leading to where? Roman has no idea what lies beyond those mountains. And even if he can reach them and cross that pass, what then? Freezing to death in the bitter cold of the continent's barren interior seems the only possibility.

"Kill it," says Trent, and it takes Roman a moment to realise what he means. In the meantime, he runs over another mound, feels it crunch and collapse like a pumpkin struck by a hammer. He squeezes the brakes and cuts the engine.

Trent dismounts as Brock comes up, his snowmobile rattling violently as he bounces on the black shapes. Brock stops, shooting Roman a look like it's his fault the ride has been so uncomfortable.

"This is the route I take every day," says Roman, holding up his hands helplessly. Brock dismounts, pulling his rifle around on its sling to point at Roman one handed, the other rubbing his numb butt.

"No need for that," Trent says distractedly, pushing the rifle's barrel aside without looking up, as if he has a monopoly on threatening Roman with guns and isn't in the mood for it just now. He doesn't seem much interested in Roman nor Brock, instead inspecting the mounds.

"We didn't get far," says Brock, looking back towards the base, a blocky outline hugging the horizon.

"No, we didn't." Trent kicks one of the mounds. It's a very dark green and covered in cracks like a dry creek bed. "You know what this is, right?"

Brock shrugs. "A mossy rock?"

"That's not moss," says Roman with dawning realisation. "It's scales."

Trent nods. He goes down on his haunches and uses his gloved finger to prise apart a section of the mass jutting from the slushy ice, opening a folded flap of leathery flesh in its surface. "Look here."

With sick fascination, Roman crowds in behind him.

And stares into the glassy eye of a dinosaur.

12

"The field of velociraptors," says Trent. He releases the eyelid, but the eye remains open, fixated on the men as if they're responsible for imprisoning the creature in ice all these long years. The eyeball is a khaki-coloured orb cut through with a dark slit, encased in a translucent lens like a cat's eye marble. A crust of frosted rime clouds its perfect surface, although meltwater runs from the corner of the eye like tears.

"They're thawing out, coming apart like everything else around here," says Roman, his mind going back to the cave with the Tyrannosaurus, the glimpse of movement and the water running from the ice.

"Well, that will make it easier for us to take their blood," says Brock.

"Or for them to take ours," says Roman, glancing around superstitiously, expecting one of the creatures to be looming over his shoulder. Instead, something much more dangerous crowds in on him, Trent breathing down his neck.

"Time to go. These will keep," he says, pointing at the velociraptors.

"In this heat?" says Roman. He glances up at the sun and then down at the ice. Both are blindingly bright, one reflecting the light of the other. His vision swims, making everything look like it is melting, and quickly. Sweat gathers inside his clothes, so that he feels that even he is defrosting after a long time locked in the ice.

"It's still Antarctica. You know of anything which truly thaws out here?" says Trent.

Roman feels emboldened by the changing conditions, his blood growing hot. "I've never seen the coast collapse like that before. Parts of it, yes, bits and pieces, but the whole stretch like that?"

"That was… unexpected," concedes Trent, a trace of concern shimmering over his stern features.

"You didn't time your attack to correspond with it?"

"No, we timed it to ambush the supply ship, of course! Now that's fucked and we're playing catch up. But I know one thing. We need the blood to barter for food, ammunition, and most of all, for leverage. I need this chip in play to have any chance of us living through the month."

"Sounds like you've gone off half-cocked."

Trent grabs Roman by the collar and pulls him close. His breath smells of fish and cigarettes. "Are you questioning me, you little—"

"Shit!" says Brock, jumping on the spot in fright. He reflexively fires his rifle with a bang which echoes around the tundra like a boomerang of sound, startling the other two men. Recovering quickly, Trent throws Roman to the ground and whips his pistol out of its holster, scanning for threats. The wind howls, whipping at his clothes as he turns, but otherwise there is no movement or sound, no sign of an attack.

On the ground, Roman's face is right next to an unpleasant sight—the pulped head of a velociraptor. With its split green skin and gory red insides spattering the slushy ice, it looks like a burst watermelon dropped from a height. Brock shot it point-blank.

"What'd you do that for?" growls Trent when he realises what has happened. He lowers his pistol but keeps it ready, as if deciding whether to shoot Brock.

"Damn thing blinked!" protests Brock, jabbing his rifle at the bloody mess, which, unfortunately for Roman, means the weapon is also pointed at him.

He scrabbles to his hands and knees and crawls back towards the shelter of the snowmobile. There he is confronted with a similar, horrifying scene of scattered remains where he's crushed the velociraptor's head beneath the vehicle's tracks. In his head, the macabre scene in the cafeteria runs in like a horde of blood-drenched demons, a vision of hell to haunt him for the rest of his life. Dead bodies dance on strings, pulled by a red devil he can only glimpse at, high above, burning inside the sun. It's pulling him too, not up, but down, into the true hell of burning cold among the ice. He screams.

Trent spins, pistol aimed at Roman, but he can't stop screaming, his nerves snapped.

"I want a gummy," he wails around panting breaths. What he really wants is to go home, but he can't so he craves the only space of refuge he's been able to carve out of this nightmare. He doesn't care how pathetic he looks, or sounds; no one and nothing else matters except the rush towards oblivion. He seeks darkness, with everything blotted out, so he curls into a foetal ball, blubbering and shrieking in turns, desperately desiring a release from the existential terror which has caught up with him, only ever kept at bay through the drugs and despondency, and then only temporarily.

How he wishes he were on the cliffs right now; he'd throw himself off and be done with it. The voice in his head is a shrill cry, an insistent demand to end it all. Roman hates himself for this weakness, wanting to be stronger, disappointed that he's not.

"Will you shut the fuck up?" says Trent, and when Roman doesn't—he can't hear him above the devil shrieking in his mind—the man stomps over in gruff annoyance and pistol-whips him across the head.

Roman's whole reality freezes, his vision an error screen which jolts a few inches to one side and then goes black. When it reboots an indeterminate time later, it flickers back to life, his eyes blinking rapidly. He doesn't know where he is, but he suspects it's the hell he fears. It is cold, a bitter freezing cold which burns, with the howl of the wind the voice of the devil, promising a slow, agonising descent deeper into this infinite pit of misery and ice. He feels engulfed by pain, wrapped up by the frigid embrace of the ocean, his death finally come.

Roman breathes out, expecting to see bubbles through water. Instead, it is mist which escapes him, as if his soul is leaving his body, fleeing the unbearable agony it has had to stand, residing inside his weak flesh. In this mist, he sees blurry figures, two men perhaps, though perhaps not, their flapping arms like the dark wings of angels. If they are angels, they are evil and malicious, wishing him ill. They prod downwards with silent spears of light, cavorting around and jabbing at other shapes around their feet—disembodied heads. These heads writhe and buck, sinners buried up to their necks, trapped in the ice but desperate for freedom.

Just like Roman.

Bleary, he tries to sit up. There is frantic shouting laying siege to his eardrums, but something is keeping this sound at bay. He fishes inside his ears with fingers made too fat with gloves, yet still manages to clear enough of the slushy snow to hear better.

"Fucking things are coming to life," says one of the blurry figures, only slowly coming into focus. Roman can't remember who they are, though he can see now that they're humans. This does little to allay his fear of them, their anger radiating off them like heat waves. He flinches but can't escape as one lays their insistent hands on him, dragging him somewhere he doesn't want to go with a grip like claws.

"No," says Roman, but is ignored. Nothing he wants ever seems to matter, and right now all he wants in the world is to lie back down and return to the land of sleep, with delicate snowflakes falling on his face and sealing up his eyes. His breath is frigid in his lungs, the air coarse and moving sluggishly. He doesn't have the strength to rise.

"Get up or they'll fucking eat you!" says the man. His frost-filled beard makes him look like some type of horrifying yeti. Roman knows he's going to carry him to a cave somewhere, and there he will be eaten anyway. So why not die here?

He's picked up under the armpits like a hunk of meat, dead weight to be dragged and slung over the back of a vehicle. He lands across it with a limp flop, feeling nothing and happy about that fact, the bite of the cold preserving him even as the warmth of some radiant being makes everything weightless and airy.

Bright light stabs his retinas and is followed near instantaneously by an equally brilliant sound. It is the spears; they are striking the sinners, although what these have done to deserve such a treatment, Roman doesn't know. It must be something terrible, because God, or some equally powerful deity, has transformed them into hideous reptiles. They fight their way free of their icy prisons of torment, cold violence in their eyes.

The dark angel, his wings no more than frantically waving arms, devoid of their feathers, throws his spears and these cut through the reptile beings, who do not die easily, or silently, thrashing and roaring as their limbs are torn off, their bodies thrown to the ground.

"Go, go!" says the angel. Its shadowy form quickly melts away in the heat of combat. All that remains is the fragile man beneath. It is Brock, no angel. His gun spits bright defiance, but the spears are not divine retribution, only mundane bullets, evil metal to snuff out life, or to bring blessed release. Roman finds himself longing for their touch. But it is not to be, the vehicle beneath his belly roars. The reptiles—velociraptors, Roman remembers their name, and he shudders—roar in return and give chase as the snowmobile shoots away. They snap at Roman's face as it hangs close to the blur of passing ice and he flinches, his unconscious reflexes wanting to live even if he does not.

Brock uses the distraction to mount his own vehicle, tearing up the tundra in the wake of Trent and Roman as they rev their snowmobiles to top speed, outpacing even the swift velociraptors which trail in their wake, disoriented and sluggish from their revivification.

13

The two snowmobiles skid to a halt before a yawning black hole in the ice. It is like a great mouth, the tundra itself opening wide to swallow them whole. Huge stalactites and stalagmites line its rim, looking like massive, sharp teeth. Meltwater drips down their lengths like saliva, completing the illusion of a beast, hungry for their flesh.

"This is it," says Roman, nursing the great lump on his head, his skull ringing like a struck bell.

"Took your bloody time finding it," says Brock with a stretch and a yawn.

Roman slithers from the seat. "Well, if Trent didn't whack me with his pistol, I might not have been in such a daze for so long."

"You were hysterical," says Trent, swinging his leg up and over the snowmobile like a rugged cowboy dismounting his horse. He tugs up his belt and shifts it around to bring the holster within easy reach.

"He's always hysterical," says Brock. "Remind me why we need him again, now we're here?"

"There's a reason I kept you alive, isn't there?" Trent asks Roman.

"To prolong my suffering?" says Roman, walking towards the controls for the cable car, a bulky steel box by the entrance of the cave. Attached to it is a massive winch and cable slung overhead, and below these, a pair of steel tracks coated with sparkling rime. They lead into the dark abyss at a steep angle, quickly disappearing in the gloom.

"He's a bit touchy because we killed all his friends," says Trent.

"I didn't know he had any friends," says Brock.

"I thought you were my friend for a minute there," Roman says to Trent as the other two join him by the cave. "But you just wanted to steal the blood I harvested."

"Kept you out of the fight, didn't it? You're alive, aren't you?" says Trent.

"Don't do me any more favours."

"Okay, you got it. That's the last time I save your life. It doesn't mean you don't owe me one, though."

"Oh, a favour for a favour, is that it? I'm meant to pay you back, and for what, framing me so that I get locked up for days? Give me a break. I've brought you here. What you want is down there." Roman points into the dark void, a shudder running down his spine. He remembers the Tyrannosaurus waiting in the ice, the biggest he's ever seen, and he isn't keen to make its acquaintance again. Not if there's even the slightest possibility of... His thoughts trail off as they butt up against something he doesn't want to face, but must.

"Those velociraptors," he begins.

"That was *crazy*," says Brock.

"You would think it impossible, right?"

"For them to come back to life?" says Trent distractedly, wiping the frost from the cable car control with his glove. "What am I, a palaeontologist?"

"You're a geologist, though, aren't you?"

Trent shoots him a hard look. "You been in my file?"

"You've been in mine, I'm sure. Otherwise, you wouldn't have singled me out as your Tyrannosaurus gopher."

Trent grunts with a nod, returning his attention to the controls. He turns a switch to the right. The cable above them jerks into life with a shrill squeal as the winch engages. The cable moves less than a metre before it comes to a juddering halt. The winch's cry rises to a tortured shriek, as if the machine is in agony. The whole rig rattles violently. Trent quickly returns the switch to neutral.

"You know how to work this thing, don't you?" he says to Brock.

"*I* was an engineer," Brock says with a proud jab of a thumb into his chest, as if anyone asked.

"*Was* being the operative word. The same as I *was* a geologist, before these bastards kidnapped me." Trent kicks the steel rig holding up the winch, as if, in its role as infrastructure, it symbolises those who had brought them to Antarctica under false pretences.

Roman frowns. "Wait, they *kidnapped* you?"

"From another Antarctic base, an American one which head-hunted me from the mines in Queensland."

"Same with me," says Brock. "The US base, not the Aussie mines. I came to the continent after working back home in the states."

"So, you two knew each other before… all this."

"Yes."

"And where is this Yank station?"

Trent shrugs and motions vaguely at the horizon. "As far as I can tell, it's beyond those mountains, though you know what it's like around here, everything looks the same."

"I suppose they blindfolded you?"

"More like drugged us, had the doc pronounce us dead, and shipped us here in coffins, if you can believe it!" says Brock, fiddling with the controls but getting no better results.

"Your families think you're dead, then?"

Brock's face twists into a grimace, unhappy to be reminded of something he'd prefer not to think about.

"No one to miss you?" sneers Roman, twisting the knife in the wound. He's rewarded with Brock turning away, the sunlight glistening in moist eyes. Trent puts a reassuring hand on the man's shoulder. He nods down at the control panel, indicating for him to focus on the task at hand, before he turns to Roman to answer his question.

"I have a daughter back in Australia, and yes, I assume she believes I'm dead," he says, icy steel in his words. "But I'm getting out of here and back to her, even if I have to wade through an ocean of blood."

"Seems that's entirely what it will take," says Roman. "You've seen what they do to intruders, right? It won't be long before they figure out what's happened and come for us."

"Let me worry about that."

"I'll reserve my rights to worry about what I want."

"Well, worry about how we're going to get down into the cave, because this thing is gummed up," says Brock, wiping away his tears with one hand, angrily flicking the controls with the other. It sets the winch screaming once more, the cable straining but not moving.

"Must be iced up down there," says Trent, peering into the cave for some glimpse of the cable car.

Roman splashes his boot in a slushy pool of melted ice. Water trickles down into the cave in rivulets. “You think that’s very likely?”

“It’s colder down there than up here.”

Roman doesn’t mention what he saw in the cave earlier, the flutter of movement in the Tyrannosaurus’s foot. He tries to forget it himself, but the visceral fear shudders through his body anyway, a subconscious thought drifting through his guts. He glances over his shoulder, fully expecting to see the velociraptors have caught up, but there is nothing but the limitless white plain of the tundra, hazy with reflected sunlight. The wind howls like an unseen predator waiting just beyond the horizon.

“With the cable car out of service, what do we do?” asks Brock, edging away from the cave as if he knows what is coming next.

“We go down,” says Trent, his words cold as the grave. To Roman’s ears, they are the pronouncement of a death sentence.

14

Entering the cave is to leave the land of the living, where light makes everything easier to bear, and be engulfed in darkness, swallowed by the icy earth, forgotten and dead, a morsel to be devoured by an infinite hunger which is never sated. The jaws of the cave mouth slowly shut as they recede into the distance, a tiny circle of light growing smaller as the three men descend into the guts of something older than time.

Soon it is gone completely, the light of the sun replaced by the meagre substitute of headlamps. The beams dance around, pointing like ghostly fingers at this and that as the men twist their heads, trying to illuminate everything all at once. But it is impossible, and as soon as their backs are turned, the shadows rush in on them from behind, hiding who knows what dangers.

It is easy to populate these blank spaces with monsters, for this is a realm of monsters, where men are little more than parasites. They are mosquitoes, seeking to push their proboscises into larger creatures, suck a portion of blood to sustain them and hope they don't get crushed in the process.

The only reminder which Roman, Trent, and Brock have of the surface world of men is the cable, taut as a hangman's rope above their heads, and the steel tracks they shimmy down, a meagre symbol of humanity's hubris, plunging into the depths to guide their way. Their gloves slough rime from the steel as they slide down, inch by inch, wary of falling. Even with the callipers of their boots digging into the ice, the ground is treacherous, the slope steep and freshly refrozen water runoff from above making everything slick.

Roman is having a harder time than the other two, forced to carry the blood extraction gear in a large backpack. He would protest, but the automatic rifle—the only encumbrance Brock carries—is enough to silence him. Trent also has only a minimal burden, his backpack sagging, filled only with empty plastic sacks, ready to receive their vampire's portion of blood. Climbing back out of here, with all that extra weight, will be an altogether more difficult task, but one Roman hopes to experience, because it means he'll be leaving this place alive. It's all he can hope for, and even if his life is measured in brief moments of terror, his body sings, vibrating with vitality in a way it hasn't in a long time. For a while, he tells himself it is the withdrawal from eating so many gummies, but no, it is something else, an even more powerful drug.

Adrenaline.

***

"Well, that's not a good sign," says Brock as they reach the bottom of the tracks.

Roman can't help but agree. The way is blocked by a twisted lump of torn metal. It's the cable car, utterly wrecked and useless. It rocks gently on the taut cable, like a corpse hanging from the end of a rope, swaying in a breeze. But there is no breeze down here, the air frigid and painful to breathe, which makes the other thing they're looking at utterly baffling. The destroyed car sits in a foot of water.

"What's done this?" says Brock, tentatively putting his boot on part of the wreck. It creaks under his weight, shifting like uncertain ground. Wincing, he steps back and points up at the cable. It catches the light from his headlamp, stiff as a garrotte wire around their throats. "That's intact, so it didn't snap, sending the car plummeting. I guess it could still fall if the brakes were disengaged, but someone would have to do that on purpose."

"Is there anyone missing?" asks Roman.

"What?"

"Like, were you keeping track of who you were slaughtering up there on the surface? Was anyone absent?"

"It all happened a bit fast to take a headcount," says Trent.

"You mean body count."

"We just kept shooting until no one was shooting back," says Brock.

"That accounts for the soldiers," says Roman. "But what about all the other… workers?" He is reluctant to use the word slave, not wanting to admit to himself that that's what he was too, and still is, only with a change in masters.

"Some fish might have slipped through the net," admits Trent.

Roman's guts twist to hear his fellow human beings referred to as such, and it takes him a second to realise the feeling is a pang of guilt that he's one of the survivors of their bloody purge.

"We're only worried about who's with us. Everyone else," says Brock, looking meaningfully at Roman, "is an enemy."

Roman ignores him, his residual fear too high in this place to feel extra from the likes of Brock, gun or no gun. "So, it's possible there was a team out?" he asks Trent.

"No," Trent replies. "I'm not that stupid. I checked the roster."

"Perhaps someone moonlighting, then? The black market, remember?"

Trent grunts.

"Doesn't explain why the car's all smashed up," says Brock. He shines his light through the buckled frames which were once windows. "Especially without any bodies inside."

"Could be they climbed out?" suggests Roman.

"And what, wandered around the tundra with a broken leg?"

"Velociraptors probably got them if that's the case," says Trent, his voice black with gallows humour. He smiles. "It doesn't matter, though, does it?"

"I think it matters a lot," says Roman. "Whatever happened to them could happen to us."

"You work down here. What could happen to them?"

Roman looks around as if checking if anyone is listening. He leans in close, whispering. "Tyrannosaurus," he says. The word mists in the air and hangs there like a manifestation of dread.

"Tyrannosaurus?" says Brock, his oafish voice far too loud. "That's what we've come for."

Roman grimaces, superstitious that such a loud invocation of the monster will bring it to life. In his mind he sees it twitching, breaking free of the ice. He can't tell if the roar in his ears is real or just the rush of his blood as his heart beats frantically.

"I'm more worried about getting around this bloody thing," Trent says pragmatically, his headlamp's beam playing over the wrecked cable car.

"Guess we'll have to go back," suggests Roman, his thoughts screaming at him, not liking the look of the smashed car one bit. He shines his headlamp on huge scrapes in the metal, probably where the car struck rocks, but to him, they could just as easily be the score marks of giant teeth.

“There’s nothing for it. We have to climb over,” says Trent.

“I wouldn’t want to be the first to try it,” says Brock.

“No need to risk our own necks when we have this canary in the coalmine.” Trent’s headlamp points at Roman.

With his facial features hidden in shadow, and the shining circle of the lamp a single baleful eye, Trent looks like an inhuman Cyclops, hungry for blood. Roman’s pulse pounds in his veins, the pressure so high he thinks he’s about to spring a leak, the precious fluid draining from his body and sold on the black market to other monsters like the one before him. But the leak isn’t from his body, and he can hear it. It’s water, a thin cascading stream coming from the ice walls of the cave and pouring into the pool beyond the cable car, like the world has sprung a leak.

“I don’t think it’s safe,” says Roman lamely.

Brock laughs and jabs him with the muzzle of his rifle. “I think that’s the point of you going first.”

Roman tries to swallow. There’s a lump in his throat, clogging it. He fights to push it down, but is afraid to succeed, as if it’s holding back a great dam of liquid. He looks at the walls. They creak as if under pressure. Cracks glint in the passing beam of his headlamp and he can’t be sure if more are forming or not, though he can hear them in his ears, slight clicks which itch at his eardrums like the chirp of hidden insects.

“Go on, Roman,” says Trent. “We didn’t spare you for nothing.”

“I thought it’s because I can siphon Tyrannosaurus blood,” says Roman. “If I die, then what will you do?”

“We’ll give it our best crack. Better that than dead. As I said, I’ve got a daughter to get back to. You got any kids, by the way?”

“No, but I’m somebody’s kid. My parents don’t know if I’m alive or dead.”

“You mean, if I blow your brains out here and now, it doesn’t make any difference?” asks Brock.

“It’ll make a difference to me.”

“And none to me,” says Trent. “Now get. Sooner you’re across, the sooner we’re on our way.”

“What if I climb over and run away?”

Trent and Brock both laugh. The mocking sound echoes down the cave and comes back, the joke on them, too, all of them in the same shit.

"If you could run, then you would have done so a long time ago," says Trent with the knowing smile of a convict locked away in a prison from which it's impossible to escape.

"Do you even have an exit strategy?"

"Why, what's yours?" says Brock. "The coward's way out?"

"Ironically, I never gathered up the courage to go through with it."

"Suicide is nothing glamorous," says Trent. "We've all considered it. But no, if I'm going to die, I'm going to go down swinging."

"You'll fight your way out?"

"I prefer to negotiate."

"Then why the thirst for blood?"

"I prefer to negotiate from a position of strength."

"You don't strike me as much of a negotiator."

Trent reaches for the butt of his pistol. Roman sighs. Laying a hand on the side of the cable car, he begins to climb.

15

The creaking and rocking of the cable car is terrifying, but the ice-slick surface is what really sets Roman on edge, his hands and feet slipping and skidding as he makes his way across the shattered mass of metal. A single misstep and he'll fall. He holds on tight, but it's not like the structure is stable either. There's the constant threat the cable car simply collapses beneath him. In that case he's more afraid he'll be hideously wounded as the twisted cube of metal rolls on top of him.

Roman is sure Brock and Trent would simply step past him without a word, leave him to slowly bleed out in terrible agony. He'll more likely freeze to death, a small consolation, as the numbing embrace of the cold would be a blessed release from pain and worry. Perhaps he'll even be preserved in the ice for some future generation of explorers to dig free. Though, knowing his luck, it'll most likely be some super advanced race of dinosaurs, come to siphon off a portion of his blood to research the long-extinct species of Homo Sapiens.

"Hope I come back to life and bite them," he says, picturing Trent and Brock with dinosaur faces, a look of shock in their reptile eyes as the feral human springs from the ice and runs amok.

"You across yet?" shouts Trent, unseen behind the bulk of the car.

"Just on top," Roman calls back.

"Good. Tie a rope around something sturdy. Throw one end over this way and another down the other side. It'll make it easier for us."

"That's definitely what I seem to be doing, for some unknowable reason," Roman mutters to himself as he complies with the order. He doesn't know why he's afraid of them, not when he's spent these past three years dreaming of the release of death. They would be doing him a favour, ending it quickly.

But, as his hands grasp the rope, lowering himself down the far side of the cable car, with his breath wheezing in and out of his lungs and his muscles straining, he feels more alive than he has in a long time, and he grips this feeling hard, clutching for a life which hangs by a thread.

***

His boots touch down not onto solid ice but upon melted slush which shifts under his weight. Still, it is a relief to be down off the wreck of the cable car, even as he sinks in up to his calves. His boots might be waterproof, but his clothes are only water-resistant, and while they stave off the splashes as he moves back from the rope, there is the threat of water seeping in. To get wet down here can be a death sentence, a frostbitten limb crippling.

He probes the icy slurry with his boots, fearing it will drop off at any moment. An unseen hole could swallow him in an instant. It would be like plunging into a freezing cold river, with no guarantee he could get out without help. That is if he doesn't simply sink so deep he becomes trapped in some pocket of the cave filled with water, suffocating as the sharp pain of the constricting cold drives the air from his lungs. He can imagine his numb fingers scratching at the ice, already stiff as claws, desperate for escape, his brain screaming for oxygen as he blacks out. He shudders to contemplate such a fate and decides it best to stand still.

***

After a heated argument between Trent and Brock which ends abruptly with a sound like meat being whacked with a tenderising mallet, Roman hears one of them climbing over, the way made quicker for having a rope to hold on to. The whole structure of the cable car rattles violently under their weight, and Roman can't help but shuffle away from it uneasily.

Caught between the looming potential of a crushing death and the blind abyss of unknown ground behind him, he feels one is the more obvious danger. The twisted and torn metal edges of the car catch the light of his headlamp like the spikes of a torture device. He can feel these pressing into his flesh, although the sharp pains are actually phantoms of the cold. He hugs himself; to bring him comfort as much as relief.

"You're getting out of here," he tells himself, not really believing it. He wants to run, but to where? He can now go only deeper, the way out blocked by this great hunk of metal he fears. Behind him is an unknowable abyss. What waits for him there? He knows, and he shivers with more than the cold.

A splash brings him from his introspective reverie, Trent landing next to him. He untangles himself from the rope.

"Piece of piss," Trent says to Roman, icicles twinkling like stars in his beard. He then shouts back over the car. "Alright, you cry baby. Your bloody turn."

"Trouble in paradise?" says Roman.

"Nothing a punch in the face won't cure. Brock has his uses but he's a bit of a dumb beast, if you know what I mean. He needs herding."

"That's what we are to you, then? Cattle?"

"Brock's a bull in a china shop, that's for sure," says Trent with a single bark of laughter. It echoes back at them like a repeating gunshot. Roman looks around, wary of them drawing attention. The walls shudder with barely restrained violence, as if the cave itself wants to kill them, angry at their intrusion.

"Careful," Roman warns, watching a spreading spiderweb of cracks form.

"Defending Brock now, are we? That's ironic," says Trent, planting his hands on his hips. "Don't forget he'd have gunned you down with the rest. It's me who protected you."

"Will you shut up?"

"Don't tell me—"

"Whoa, easy there!" says Brock. Roman looks up in disbelief to see the man at the apex of the cable car, one hand on the rope tied to its top, the other waving around in the air as he rides the destroyed vehicle like a cowboy on a rogue horse. It shifts and slides beneath his feet, and it's hard to tell whether he's moving with the vehicle's motion, or unbelievably, purposefully rocking it back and forth.

Roman's eyes dart across the cable car, his sight catching on every sharp piece of metal. He feels the stabbing pains again, the jagged metal barbs piercing him like an ice pick striking the walls of the caves. He feels fragile, cracks forming on his skin, the thin barrier covering him breaking, first slow then fast, his blood gushing forth in an explosive wave. This premonition of his death unfolds before his eyes as he sees the inevitable come to be.

He steps back quickly, uncaring of what lies behind him. Trent does the same, for they both sense what's next. The cable car lurches with a sick jolt of shrieking metal and comes rushing towards them like an avalanche.

16

Brock screams as he tumbles, sliding down the roof of the cable car. He is hurled from it, a test dummy thrown from a car wreck, his body limp as he strikes the cave wall and falls. Trent and Roman scream too, running as the car comes crashing down where they had been a moment before. It throws up a wave of water which Roman avoids like acid, clambering up a stalagmite as if shimmying up a tree trunk.

Trent disappears, obscured by the cable car as it rolls once more and then pauses to balance upright precariously. It shudders and sways, unsure of which way to fall. It looms over Roman like a monster, ready to crush him. He pumps frantic breaths out through pursed lips, absurdly trying to blow it in the opposite direction. With agonising slowness, like a shifting glacier, the great metal mass begins to sag under its own weight. Crumpling in half, its top portion leans to the left, and the whole overbalances. Resembling nothing more than a massive pickaxe, the car strikes forward and rips into the cave wall with a *shunk*.

For a second nothing more happens. For a second Roman thinks he is safe.

He is wrong.

The ice wall shudders, a web of cracks shooting out in all directions from the point of impact. Then an explosion like the shattering of a glass aquarium. A wave of water bursts forth from the rupture.

And in it are dinosaurs.

***

They're stegosauruses, a whole herd of them. They cascade out of the wall and flop into the cave like fish thrown up on the beach by a wave, a monstrous tonnage of flesh. Their bodies are bulbous, fat around the torso, yet long, tapering to a tiny head at one end and a spiked tail at the other. Rows of bony plates line their backs. Normally used for protection, these become lethal weapons, gouging huge chunks of flesh from each other's flanks as the mass of dinosaurs spill forth, packed tightly together. Some of the bone plates from different creatures interlock and grind together, a grating sound like stone on stone.

With a wet slap the dinosaurs land in a great, chaotic heap, but they do not sit still. They bellow and thrash, confused revenants reborn into a world of pain after long stasis in a frozen purgatory. In their distress and agony, they lash out with their tails. The four spikes there are dedicated weapons and can deal real damage. Stunned, and not that bright to begin with, the stegosauruses don't care if those they hurt are their own kind, self-interested defence the only thing on their tiny, panicked brains as the tails strike like spiked war-maces, pulping flesh and piercing organs. The water runs red with their blood, and the air fills with the stink of punctured intestines. Roman climbs further up his stalagmite to escape not only these but the wash of polluted water lapping at its base.

The stegosauruses struggle to rise. Most are gravely injured, the rest disorientated. Those which do manage to get up are woozy on their feet, stumbling as if drunk, blood oozing from wounds, peering around blindly out of tiny eyes set in tiny heads.

One of them stumbles past the base of Roman's icy perch, turns its head up to look at him, as if he has any answers for it. Roman feels pity for it, his heart going out to such a dumb beast in distress. He sees the pain in its sparkling eyes as he shines his headlamp into them, and the stegosaurus blinks myopically. Roman can't tell if it sees him or not, if it senses in him a threat, but the dinosaur doesn't act aggressively towards him, its bony tail limp, as if it doesn't have the strength to lift it. Exhausted, the stegosaurus leans its bulk on the stalagmite, and the ice pillar creaks under its immense weight.

"Meaning me harm or not, this thing is going to get me killed anyway," says Roman, digging in his callipers and hugging tighter. Startled by the sound of his voice, the stegosaurus jumps on the spot, a comical movement for such a big creature. It looks up at Roman again with new sight, watching him with those wet bovine eyes. Heart beating hard, Roman takes a few deep breaths, and manages to calm down a little, seeing here a harmless herbivore. But then he is startled himself by a hard, loud sound, and nearly loses his grip and falls.

He's looking straight at the dinosaur as the head of the stegosaur explodes, gore rupturing from its split skull. The huge body slumps as the legs buckle. The bang of the gunshot reverberates in the confined space of the cave, the echo bouncing around like a lethal ricochet which panics the herd.

Then everything really goes to hell.

17

The wet slap of hot gore from the stegosaurus's head splashes Roman's face. The shock is so great, the sensation so intense, that for a moment he believes he's been shot himself. Phantom pain rushes across his skin, adrenaline burning like fire in his veins. His fingers lose their strength and his callipers skid and slip from the ice.

He falls backwards and lands with a hard thump.

There is no splash of water, no being submerged in the cold embrace of slushy ice. His fall is far too short, and he bounces upon leathery firmness. He reflexively flails his arms, feeling gravity pulling at him, threatening that he falls further. His forearms strike something hard, jarring the bone. The skin is grated away—even through his clothes—by an abrasive surface as his arms slide down it, terminating with his gloved hands grabbing a rounded edge. They lock on as he is bucked up in the air and lands once more, the impact driving the breath from his lungs with a bestial grunt. The sound is echoed from nearby, much louder, and he feels the surface beneath him pumping like a bellows.

The shock of the gunshot is shaken from him, replaced by disorientation to find himself unhurt, yet being rattled around vigorously. He looks around, frantically trying to figure out where he is, but his view is blocked by the thing he holds, and more like it all around in a pair of tight, overlapping rows. They hem him in like the rocks of a tight gulley. The ground beneath him is cracked into segments, resembling a riverbed long ago dried up. But it pulses with life, and the whole environment heaves.

The noise is overwhelming, a monstrous, honking hoot repeating from many throats, and the pounding of huge feet splashing through the melted ice. They are sounds of distress, and Roman begins to understand. More gunfire lights up the cave, and he sees what he's holding resembles bone, bleached white with age, the surface porous and rough.

It's the back plate of a stegosaurus. He's riding a dinosaur.

His callipers scratch its tough, scaly hide for purchase and he pushes himself up, holding onto the plate for dear life, bracing against a fall which he's aware will kill him.

Because he's in the middle of a stampede.

***

Roman's headlamp provides little illumination of the chaos. Everywhere he looks is a sea of heavy, undulating flesh and waving bone plates; these are the terrible teeth and scaly gums of some impossible monster, seeking to rip him limb from limb. To fall is to be made into mincemeat by this organic threshing machine, his body then pulverised to paste beneath the pounding hammers of the dinosaur's stomping feet.

The flashes of gunfire seem to be coming from everywhere and nowhere, illuminating the cave ceiling like distant lightning among clouds. His own meagre headlamp beam flails about as he clings on to his precarious perch, unable to orientate himself. He has no idea where he is headed or which way safety might lie. The terror he feels opens wide to consume him, a yawning abyss of panic at his helplessness. An adrenaline surge sings through his body like an injection of hot liquid, tightening his grip and tensing his body. It's a reflexive, subconscious response; there is no time to think, no plans to make. All he can do is hang on and hope for the best.

It doesn't help that the stegosauruses are as terrified and confused as he is. They are running from a threat, their tiny minds acting in unison, the gunfire a goad which keeps them moving. If only it would cease, then this mad dash would also cease, and Roman could climb down. It barely crosses his mind that whoever is firing is also doing so out of fear, or that once set in motion, the stampede is something which is unstoppable.

Bullets whack into flesh with a wet sound like a rock dropped in mud. Others ricochet off bony plates with whickering whines and dazzling sparks. Roman ducks his head down behind their cover as more shots zip past his ears and stitch down the plates, making them vibrate in his hands. He hears bullets sucked into the quagmire embrace of densely packed organs with a slurping sound, accompanied by a shrill note of distress blown through a war horn, a creature sounding the retreat in the face of defeat.

Roman feels as much as hears these changes—the air pulsing through the body beneath him, the lopsided tilt of its gait—and he realises it's the dinosaur he's riding which has been hit.

Fresh terror explodes in his brain as he fears it will topple, throwing him clear to land among the pulping hooves. Instead, it merely turns hard, angling away from the pain, and Roman is forced to wrap both his arms and legs around a plate as it tilts like a sailing ship taking a new bearing.

Then he sees it: the flickering light of a headlamp. A brief respite of relief flutters through Roman's dark thoughts to see it. It is a beacon of hope, a sign of human life, of possible rescue. If nothing else, it is something to anchor himself to, a way to orientate himself in this madness. Unable to control the stegosaurus, Roman finds he doesn't have to. The dinosaur is heading towards it, like an insane captain steering for a lighthouse, hoping to wreck itself upon the rocks.

As the monster nears the light, with Roman shining his own headlamp in that direction, he sees that they are indeed heading towards a great rock, jutting out of the water and covered in glistening rime, like an iceberg in an ocean whipped to froth by the passing of the dinosaurs either side of it. Far from slowing when confronted by this obstacle, Roman's mount, driven mad by its grievous wounds, ploughs on. Its great bellows lungs wheeze with strain and its legs pound a rhythmless tattoo. Roman is almost thrown from its back by this lopsided gait, and as the rock looms in front of them, he even considers jumping. But there is no time, the decision made for him.

The stegosaurus, blind with agony, rams directly into the rock.

There is a brittle sound accompanied by a hollow thump, like a bird's neck breaking as it flies heedless into an invisible window. The body beneath Roman crumples, the strength in the legs gone as they turn to jelly, and he is hurled forward himself, slapping against the rock's face with arms outstretched to embrace it. He bounces off it, unable to find purchase on its icy surface, but hands grab him and haul him up as the stegosaurus sinks into the stampeding hordes of its kin, there to be ground to a pulp by the heavy mallets of their legs.

It would have been a fate shared by Roman if not for his saviour. He looks up, headlamp meeting headlamp in a dazzling moment of blindness before both turn away to spare their eyes. Stars dance in Roman's vision, but he hears the voice, a string of obscenities spat through gritted teeth as they haul him up atop the rock to safety.

It's Trent.

They both fall in a heap, panting hard, though Trent still has the breath left to curse him out. Roman is unable to say anything, stunned to be alive. His mouth moves wordlessly as his vision clears; the stegosauruses are gone, swallowed by the dark shadows of the cave. They can still be heard honking and braying as they continue their flight, but the violence of their passing is over for Roman, and he can only shake his head in wonder to have escaped it.

The gunfire has ceased, too, replaced by a more ominous sound of violence. From somewhere in the dark distance of the cave's depths comes a monstrous roaring.

18

A tremor of icy chill rattles down Roman's spine at the noise and then shoots back up again, spiking panic in the base of his brain as the roaring doesn't cease, growing in volume and fury.

"Christ," says a voice from below. "What's that?"

Roman, already on a knife's edge of tension, jumps on the spot with an involuntary squeak. The callipers of his boots skitter across the slippery rock and he almost falls. Trent, also surprised, throws out a hand to steady him, though only one. The other drops to the butt of his pistol, still in its holster, which means Trent wasn't the one doing the shooting.

"What do you think it is, you fucking idiot?" Trent says, shining his headlamp down at the owner of the voice, a revenant come back from the dead. Dripping wet and limping heavily, with blood streaming from a cut in his forehead, Brock steps into the light.

"Probably a dinosaur," he says, shouting over the sound of the continuous roaring. It's interspersed with the honking and braying of the stegosauruses and it's not hard for Roman to guess what's happening.

It's not just any dinosaur down there, but *the* dinosaur. And it's hunting, giving chase to the stegosauruses. The booming tread of many heavy feet is like thunder in the distance, echoing up out of the depths of the cave and fading as the storm travels further from them.

"Genius of the year award over here," says Trent, his hand still on his pistol, as if he's contemplating putting a dumb beast out of its misery. Roman wouldn't complain. Brock has his automatic rifle clutched loosely in one hand. It was he who set the stampede going, firing wildly into the stegosauruses, nearly getting Roman killed.

"Give us a hand getting down," Trent says to Brock.

Brock shakes his head, shrugs with a single shoulder. The other hangs limp, the joint dislocated. "Can't."

"What are you good for then?" snarls Trent, sitting down and bracing with his hands. He slides off the rock and lands with a splash.

"I shot at least one of the buggers," Brock replies. He jerks his head at the stegosaurus carcasses, and there's more than one, though it's hard to tell in the gloom which were killed by their own kind in the violent crush and which from bullets.

"And what did you do a fool thing like that for?" says Trent. "You nearly killed *us*."

"One of them was going for Roman. I was saving him."

"Don't drag me into this," says Roman, awkwardly sliding down from the rock on his belly. He nearly goes head over heels as he lands, but Trent catches him.

"Careful," says Trent. "You wouldn't want to get as wet as this stupid mongrel. You'll freeze to death."

"It's warm," says Brock.

"What is?"

"The water. It's not cold. More like a hot bath."

Roman scans his headlamp across the water, catching the glistening glow of rising steam.

"What in the hell?" says Trent, ripping off a glove and crouching down to touch the surface. "He's bloody right."

Roman's stomach drops. "I think you can forget your global warming theory as to why the ice is melting."

"Why's that?" says Brock, looking blankly between the two other men. "It's warm, isn't it?"

"Yeah," says Trent, standing slowly. "But we're deep underground. This isn't global warming." He looks up at the ceiling just as a fat drop of water plunges down to splash upon his face. He grimaces and wipes it clear. "The whole cave is melting."

"And what could cause that?"

"A geothermal event."

19

"Shouldn't we turn back?" says Roman in alarm as Trent begins walking, not towards the exit, but further into the cave. Trent doesn't respond. He sloshes through the melted ice, headlamp swaying, its small light swallowed by the immensity of the darkness ahead.

"What's the matter?" sneers Brock. "Afraid of a bit of water?"

Roman looks at him like he's gone mad. With the knock on the head he's taken, it isn't out of the question. Not that he's the brightest bulb to begin with, but with the gaping gash on his forehead, and his dumb, slack expression smeared on his face like paste, he looks like a lobotomy patient, turned loose before they had a chance to stitch him up. Unfortunately for Roman, he's also holding a gun.

"I can think of three things I'm more afraid of than the water," says Roman, eyes darting from the gun to the huge hole in the wall, out of which spewed a horde of dinosaurs. He winces and ducks as another roar reverberates through the cave, shaking loose a shower of water and icicles. To Roman, it seems the whole place could come crashing down any second. Yet Trent pushes on, heading towards the roaring like some mad Captain Ahab intent on killing the monster of myth, and Brock too stupid to realise the danger. This leaves only Roman himself, too cowardly to do anything about it, except voice objections, easily ignored.

"Don't worry, little man," says Brock, hefting the gun awkwardly. "I've got your back."

Quite literally; he skirts around Roman and gives him a prod, holding the rifle one-handed. The other hangs limply, and Brock winces as it swings on its dislocated joint.

"You'd think, of all of us, you'd be the one keenest on getting out of here," says Roman, shuffling forward like a man reluctantly walking to his execution.

"I'd freeze in the wind on the surface," says Brock, shaking his head to clear the water dripping in his eyes. He stumbles, overcome with dizziness.

"You've not lost all sense of reason, then?"

“Ha! No, not yet. Here, take this for a second, will you?”

Brock holds out the rifle. Roman frowns at it in confusion. Brock shakes it impatiently. Roman extends a hand, hovering over the glistening black weight, hesitating, afraid of some type of sadistic trick. If he tries to take it, will Brock kill him, finally given the excuse he needs?

Roman feels like he’s back on the icy cliff of the coast, watching the penguins diving and trying to decide whether to throw everything away and join them. The consequences of that choice were too much then, and they’re too much now. He doesn’t want to face it—the finality of death, or worse, what to do with life—and he was happy to let the decision fall out of his hands, even if it was scooped up by the likes of Trent and Brock.

He’s annoyed to be offered agency over his own life once more. It’s too much of a burden, and he’s even more annoyed to admit to himself that he’s found some release from the mental load of his own tortured thoughts by allowing himself to be dragged along by the will of Trent, goaded by pointed guns.

He doesn’t want that terrible responsibility, doesn’t want to carry the weight or point the gun himself, deciding where to go and what to do. He’s too afraid to make the wrong choice, so others make them for him. Brock shoves the gun hard into his chest, and Roman clutches it, the barrel pointed at the ceiling, at nothing and no one. He’s no threat, and he hates himself for it.

Brock is doing something horrific, grunting with the effort, face pale with pain as he tugs at his dislocated arm. Roman can hear the bone grinding like a mortar and pestle, the gristle of ligaments straining like taut ropes about to snap.

Roman can’t stand it. His teeth grind too, his nerves snapping with electricity. He wants the torture to end. Too heavy for him, the gun’s barrel falls through an arc; the moving hand on a doomsday clock. It ticks downwards until it is level, pausing there, waiting on death to sneak up on its victim. Brock, distracted with his grim task, doesn’t notice the barrel hovering, pointed at his chest. Roman’s finger itches as it worms onto the trigger. A shadow looms, breathing heavily, the dark form expanding and contracting.

Knowing time is short, Roman’s heart hurries ahead of him, beating the final countdown. Three, two, one…

Click.

He squeezes the trigger. The shadow falls like a curtain. There is no loud bang, but there is a flash of light, cutting across his sight like a sword as death grips him in a crushing embrace. There is a roar, so close in his ear it hurts. But it is no dinosaur.

It is Trent, growling like a bear as he pins Roman's arms, squeezing the life out of him. Roman gives in, never wanting this anyway. He lets Trent crush him, helping by exhaling what he hopes is his last breath. The world swirls, three headlamps dancing in a kaleidoscope of dazzling colours as his brain is starved of oxygen. He feels weightless, and smiles vacantly. Unburdened of the heaviness of his body—Trent has hold of it, he can have it—Roman floats upwards, towards the ceiling which sags downwards, melting to engulf him.

There is a bursting release of pressure, a bubble popping over his head, and reality is like a hammer to his head. He is not on the ceiling, trying to push through its barrier to the awaiting heavens, but on the floor, dropped into its watery hell. He shrieks soundlessly, with no air to give voice to his distress, and nearly chokes as the spasm of his diaphragm draws water into his lungs. Choking and gasping, he sits up, his lungs on fire, feeling like they've been scoured red raw by sandpaper.

The gun is no longer in his hands. Trent has it.

"What the fuck do you think you're doing, giving him this?" he barks at Brock. "He was going to shoot you, you know that, right?"

"That pussy doesn't have the balls," says Brock, still wrestling with himself, jolting his arm ineffectively.

Trent checks the magazine of the rifle, popping it out of place and shining his lamp into it. "You're lucky you'd already emptied the clip shooting up the damned dinosaurs."

"I know that. I'm not an idiot," grunts Brock, struggling.

"For God's sake," says Trent, hanging the rifle from his shoulder by the strap. "You'll never get it back in like that."

He grabs Brock, rearranges their relative positions like a back-alley chiropractor, and yanks hard. Brock howls, but the joint clicks back into place.

"That'll bruise up nicely," says Trent, and, with a similar set of deft movements, draws a spare clip of ammunition from Brock's pocket and reloads the rifle with a pop, twist, and a click. He hangs it back over his shoulder. "I don't think you can handle this with your arm, but you can have my pistol if you promise not to give it to the damned prisoner."

Brock nods weakly and takes what he's given. Trent pats him on the shoulder, eliciting another yowl of pain like a stepped-on cat.

"You should put that in a sling, maybe get idiot number two here to help you," says Trent. He looks down at Roman, extending a hand. Roman takes it.

"You going to be any more trouble?" Trent snarls as he plants Roman back on his feet and yanks him in close. Roman pulls back from the hot stink of Trent's breath, but Trent leans in tighter. "You pull any shit like that again…"

He lets the threat hang, suggestive of deeper miseries yet to be inflicted. Wet, tired, and trapped deep underground with two killers in a cave that's melting; how can it get any worse? Roman isn't sure, but he trusts Trent will find a way.

As if in answer to his unspoken question, the roaring in the distance starts up again. Trent smiles evilly and jerks his head in its direction.

"After you," he says and shoves Roman out ahead.

***

The trail isn't difficult to follow. Each time the cave divides, Roman simply shines his headlamp down each branch, looking for the tell-tale signs of carnage. Stegosaurus corpses are the breadcrumbs he follows; mounds of steaming flesh quickly cooling, their blood spreading in the water like dark ink. Sloshing past each, Roman can't help but look at the terrible wounds inflicted on the creatures. While some can be easily dismissed as the work of their fellow stegosauruses in stampede, others are not so easy to imagine as the work of a herbivore.

Brock whistles appreciatively as he guides his lamp across one of these, a great chunk taken from the side of a torso, broken ribs protruding from the gory void. Organs spill from the internal cavity and bob in the water.

"Something took a bite out of this one," he says.

Roman doesn't stop, doesn't look back, the sight already imprinted on his mind like a fate he's trudging towards and can't turn away from. He pictures himself in such a state, a pathetic, slaughtered carcass, half-eaten, his gored remains left to rot. The fear which permeates this place like the cold gnaws at his guts with sharp teeth. There's pressure on his chest as his breathing becomes shallow with panic, his lungs constricted by an invisible force. No amount of resignation, no amount of willing death to come faster, for it to be over with, can prepare him for the pain he'll feel as the huge jaws of a prehistoric monster crush him, the teeth impaling his insides and ripping him open.

The blood drains from his face and he's pale as a ghost in this world of ghosts, their forms glimpsed in the walls; dinosaurs still frozen, not yet thawed and set loose, yet watching, waiting to be resurrected. His light glides across their staring eyes. They sparkle with fiery indignation, as if it is within his power to free them and yet he refuses.

But why do they want to be freed? Out here is only pain and suffering. How dearly Roman wishes to be in their place, to crawl into their frozen cocoon and be numb, safe in their eternal stasis, locked out of time; until the world wakes up, that is, something stirring in the tectonic plates beneath the coldest continent.

It's hard to believe there's molten lava flowing, deep beneath the crust of this icy hell. But it's there, and it's rising. The steam coming off the water is testament to that. It mingles with the twinkling frost in the air, each nullifying the other, so that Roman wanders in a neutral purgatory, where the living meet the dead, and he is neither, balancing along a tight rope, a monster to his front, and another behind, Trent following in his wake, seemingly immune to the horrors they pass.

"I don't want to die down here," whispers Roman—to himself, to no one.

"And you think I do?" says Trent, pushing past him impatiently. The way now is obvious, even to a blind man, which Trent must be to not see the inevitability of their death. Roman can see it, and yet he follows anyway, with nowhere else to go.

20

The last corpse they find is different. A dinosaur, yes, but a stegosaurus? No.

"It's a Tyrannosaurus," says Brock, gawping at the carcass. It's fresher than the others, a leg still twitching, and yet definitely dead, its eyes glassy orbs, staring into the great, infinite beyond, seeing nothing. Most of its blood is on the outside of its body, too; another clue that it's not going to spring back up and attack. Trent kicks the reddened water angrily.

"What a fucking waste!" he growls. "Quick, get the equipment out and we'll siphon what we can salvage from this dead lump."

"We're not worried about…?" begins Roman, trailing off as he indicates the creature's extensive wounds.

"Time is money, Roman. Get on the syringe or I'll shove it through your eye!"

Roman does as he's told. He's not used to working on defrosted dinosaurs free of ice, so he's spoiled for choice as to possible places to stick the needle.

"Stop fluffing about and shove it in its neck," says Trent, readying the containers to collect the blood. "Go straight for the jugular."

"I think someone… *something…* already beat me to it," says Roman.

"What? Another collection team?"

Roman points at the neck. "No, the jugular. It's been ripped out."

Trent inspects the savage wound. Blood pours from ragged ends of torn-off arteries. He quickly cracks open a container and holds it under the gory fountain like he's collecting water. "This is too easy. Looks like I didn't need you, after all," he says.

These words stab Roman's heart like a needle, setting it beating hard, realising his usefulness, and therefore his life, might be at an end. Desperate to prove his worth, he quickly readies the syringe, leaning against the curve of the torso to guide it between the ribs and straight into the heart.

“Hey, you’re stealing my flow!” says Trent as Roman begins to fill a container, straight from the source. It’s a more efficient system, with less spillage, and Trent doesn’t say more. Instead, he steps back, capping his container and readying another to swap out Roman’s when it’s full.

“It’s dead,” says Brock, still standing there gawping.

“Bit slow on the uptake, aren’t you?” says Trent.

“But… it was hunting the stegosauruses. That’s what it was doing, wasn’t it?”

Trent shrugs. “We assume so, from the commotion we heard.”

“So, what was hunting *it*?” asks Roman, pointing at the Tyrannosaurus’s grievous wounds.

“Nothing,” says Trent, changing containers with a slosh of thick liquid. Despite the spilt blood there’s still plenty left to drain, certainly as much as they can carry out of here; a Tyrannosaurus is a big creature.

“What did this then?” says Roman, driving the syringe deeper as if ramming home a point. He meets resistance, the heavy muscle of the dinosaur’s meaty heart as well as Trent’s stubborn refusal to face the precariousness of their situation.

“The stegosauruses, of course,” says Trent, doubling down. “There’s nothing else down here.”

This is a lie and they both know it. Roman eyes the ice walls dubiously, afraid of what monsters still remain obscured behind their frosted surfaces.

“But how did they manage to kill it?” asks Brock.

“Through weight of numbers,” says Trent, grunting with effort, putting the last of the containers in place to be filled. “Sometimes even the strongest can be brought down by the meek, given the right opportunity.”

“Something you should keep in mind,” mutters Roman as he pokes the syringe’s trailing plastic tube into the container like he’s siphoning gasoline.

“What’s that?” says Trent. There’s no hard edge in his voice, and Roman assumes he genuinely didn’t hear over manhandling a full container of sloshing blood into his backpack.

“We should keep in mind we have to carry this stuff out of here,” says Roman, jiggling the syringe around inside the monster's heart, sucking up the last of it like a slurping straw seeking the dregs of a soda.

"Don't forget what this stuff is worth," says Trent.

"To you, maybe. You're the one cashing in."

"It buys life! Yours and mine both. Without it, we're sitting ducks, with no means to bargain, no way to get food and ammunition."

"Hold on a second, let's not change the subject," says Brock. He prods the torn throat of the Tyrannosaurus. "A thagomizer can't do that!"

Roman cocks an eyebrow at him. "Did you just use the scientific term for a stegosaurus's tail spikes?"

"It might surprise you, but I'm not stupid."

"Could have fooled me," says Trent.

"*Enough of that*," says Brock, spraying spittle from his lips. He pulls out the pistol and points it at Trent, which Roman thinks is a very stupid thing to do, but he keeps his opinion to himself.

"No more snarky comments, you hear?" continues Brock. "I'm an engineer, and I helped you overthrow the commandant, so show me some respect."

"If you're such a smart engineer," says Trent calmly, "you'd realise that, structurally, this cave is none too stable. The same goes for your aim."

Brock stiffens, offended, but sways woozily on his feet, exhausted by his injuries, his balance thrown off by his head wound. "I can hit you from here," he slurs groggily. He takes a step toward Trent for good measure.

"But if you miss," says Trent, not reaching for his own weapon, "you'll hit the ice. If it shatters, we won't have to worry about dinosaurs anymore, because we'll drown instead."

Boom!

Roman tenses, a sharp jolt of shock tightening his joints. For a second, he's sure Brock has called Trent's bluff and fired. But both Brock and Trent remain standing, their faces animated by the same shock which overwhelms Roman. The sound repeats, an ominous drum, beating at the heart of the world.

Boom. Boom. Boom.

The water shakes, the surface alive with ripples. Ice flakes drift down, knocked loose from the ceiling.

"What is that?" says Brock, no longer pointing his gun at Trent but at the walls, as if to fight them back as they collapse in upon him.

"An earthquake?" suggests Trent. The word sends a shiver of dread through all three men. The sound gets louder, not rising from the ground and the tectonic plates beneath, but along the cave, pushed at them with a movement of air which strikes Roman's face like a pulse.

"No," he says. "Something much worse."

21

His intuition running ahead of conscious thought, Roman looks at the dead Tyrannosaurus, his frantic eyes scanning the thing's scales.

"Let's get out of here," says Brock.

"Carry some of this, will you?" says Trent, hefting a backpack. Brock ignores him, limping as fast as he can away from the abyssal darkness from which the booming resounds.

"Fuck! Grab a sack, Roman," says Trent, swinging his own onto his back. The weight bends him double.

"Just a second," says Roman, wiping the scaly skin of the dinosaur like a curious palaeontologist brushing dirt from a fossil. "Oh."

"Oh? What do you mean, oh? Get the gear or we're fucked."

Roman shakes his head in horror. What he originally thought to be red and brown markings—those he'd seen on the creature when it was still frozen in the ice—turn out to be dried blood which smears away under his glove. Beneath, the Tyrannosaurus's hide is a pale green, not as dark as he remembers. And there's something else.

"These markings on the scales," he says.

Boom. Boom. Boom.

"We don't have time for this," says Trent, straining to lift the other backpack. "Leave the syringe, you'll carry more blood."

"You don't understand," says Roman, pieces falling into place, leading toward a conclusion which comes crashing down on him like a killing blow. "They're yellow."

Boom! Boom! Boom!

"I understand if you don't take this, I'll kick your head in," says Trent, forcing Roman's reluctant arms through the straps.

"No," says Roman, feeling the weight of the pack settling on his back, dragging him down. "What I'm saying is—"

Trent shoves him to get him moving. "Spit it the fuck out, but do it running."

"This isn't the same Tyrannosaurus," says Roman just before an ear-splitting roar drowns out all other sound.

***

The assaulting force of the roar nearly knocks Roman off his feet. The shockwave travels the length of the cave like a powerful gale wind, setting the ice crystals in the walls vibrating violently, threatening to collapse. Roman stumbles, spinning about, disorientated as he struggles to right himself under the weight of the blood sloshing upon his back. His headlamp twirls like a hazard light, warning of danger, but he doesn't know where it comes from, or where to run.

"Move!" barks Trent. Roman is all too happy to comply with the order, getting his feet under himself once more and slapping them into the slushy slurry of blood and melted ice. He keeps his head down, focusing on each step, fighting for balance. To fall now is to die. It's not easy to remain upright as the ground beneath him warps, waves lapping at his legs, heralding the thunderous footsteps of a looming presence. They pound his ears like hammers of the gods, growing louder each second.

"Not that way," shouts Trent, his voice receding like a Doppler effect as he flees in the opposite direction.

Roman stops dead in his tracks, frozen with terror.

Silence.

It is broken only by his heavy breathing, breath misting the beam of his headlamp.

Then a snort.

It is not him. It's too loud; a sharp punch of exhalation.

Roman slowly lifts his head, the beam of light catching on a huge silhouette in the darkness. Just as he had days before, when it was still locked in the ice, he plays the light across the shape, illuminating it section by section.

The splayed feet capped with ploughshare claws. The tree trunk legs, covered in mossy scales. The bulbous torso, rippling with muscle. Tiny arms dangling, tipped with sickle scythes. The long sweep of the tail, undulating up over a ridged spine. And, finally, the massive, blocky head, roughly hewn as if from stone. The chaotic red splash of colouration across the scales is plain to see as Roman traces the heavy brows. Beneath their deep hoods, the light glimmers as it catches on the sparkling, amber orbs of the eyes, shining like the corona of the sun, full of revived life.

Roman gulps.

This is it.

Tyrannosaurus rex.

22

Mesmerised by the shining lamp, the dinosaur doesn't charge. For a few long, agonising moments, everything seems frozen, as if the dinosaur is back in the ice, or has never left it, with Roman joining it, his limbs stiff with fright, unable to move. The only thing to indicate otherwise is the breathing of the Tyrannosaurus, its great flanks rising and falling rhythmically. Roman is too terrified to breathe, petrified of moving even the slightest muscle. There is a delicate balance in place. To turn and run will be to trigger this massive avalanche of flesh, setting off the delayed, yet inevitable, rush of violent attack.

The Tyrannosaurus tilts its head like a curious dog, as if trying to see past the light at something beyond.

Roman can hear splashing, and another light dancing on the ceiling of the cave, faint at first, but growing. The Tyrannosaurus's eyes bounce back and forth, following this movement. Its feet shift uneasily. Roman tenses, knowing the charge is coming.

He feels the terrible weight of the blood on his back, and wishes to shuck it off, to abandon this burden Trent has placed on him, aware it's going to get him killed.

The splashing behind him grows louder, and something flares in Roman's heart.

Hope.

Trent has come back for him.

No. Not for him. For the blood, Roman realises. His heart sinks under the knowledge he's not worth saving.

"Apparently *I am* an idiot," hisses a voice. It's not Trent's.

"Brock?"

"Are you going to run or what?"

Roman turns to look at the man. He's pale as a ghost, his face a waxy mask, running with sweat. Blood oozes down the side of his head, and he leans heavily to one side, favouring his good leg. The pistol is held limply, the arm dangling, as if he doesn't have the strength to lift it.

But lift it he does, because, by turning his light away, Roman has broken the spell upon the Tyrannosaurus rex.

With a bellowing roar to shake the foundations of the Earth, the monster leans its huge head forward, the whole centre of gravity shifting into a charging lunge, the hinge of the jaw swinging open to reveal the impaling spikes of teeth and pulsing purple tongue.

Bang!

The deafening primordial cry is eclipsed by the sharp, punching retorts of Brock's pistol, firing right by Roman's ear.

Bang. Bang. Bang.

Roman dumps the backpack, unwilling to die for the blood. He sees the Tyrannosaurus struck once, twice in the face with shots, carving chunks of gore and scales from its flesh. This slows it just enough for Roman to get a start running. He's keenly aware he can't outpace the long stride of the monster, but he has to try.

Brock isn't running. He can't run, only limp, and he does so, taking a step or two backwards, a futile gesture. The Tyrannosaurus is barrelling down on him, but he continues to fire. Roman casts a glance over his shoulder. The monster is so close to Brock now, the man can't help but miss with his shots.

He misses anyway, his aim sagging under the weight of the pistol; his strength spent first fleeing, then returning to save Roman.

The shots spark past the charging dinosaur.

They burrow straight into the wall of ice beyond.

***

Roman hears rather than sees the crack in the ice. It splits the air like a strike of nearby lightning. Roman flinches but keeps running. He doesn't see what happens to Brock, doesn't want to see him get eaten, afraid the sight will paralyse his limbs.

Not that anything matters, not anymore. With a huge dump of surf crashing upon a beach, a tidal wave of water erupts from the shattering wall of ice, flooding into the cave. Its roar is such to dwarf even that of the mighty Tyrannosaurus, quickly drowned out as the water engulfs everything in the cave, and Roman with it.

23

Rushing confusion, violent turmoil, and utter blindness; these are the impressions which overwhelm Roman as the water hurls him through the cave. His headlamp is gone, ripped off in the fury as the tidal wave smashes him down and picks him up, carrying him along at speeds which are so fast he seems to float, suspended in an infinite void.

In the darkness there is only the terrible sound of the turbulent torrent, a roar like the ocean heard in a shell, and a persistent, piercing pressure felt deep in his ears. These forces swirl around him like a choir of banshees, both inside and outside of his head, screaming prognostications of his death, their cries building in intensity. The voices echo his own mind, his thoughts wailing in terror, certain that this is the end.

It is the only thing he knows in his frenzied panic, and yet his body fights to survive, clawing out for someone, anyone to help him. But there is no one and nothing. He is alone in this maelstrom. If things—objects, ice, rocks, people, or dinosaurs—touch him, or he touches them, he doesn't feel it. Contact with any of these is no different than the universal force of the water, its pressure simultaneously cushioning and crushing. It holds him in its grip like a soft yet firm fist, shaking him in its fury, yet cradling him, offering mercy and release.

This paradox also manifests in the only other thing he is aware of: air, and the lack thereof. His lungs crumple like a submarine taken too deep, the internal tension building in his body until it bursts with a release of exhaled bubbles. His insides shrink; all that he is squeezed through the tube of his neck until his head grows large. There the cycle of pressure and release repeats, the pain too much as his brain screams for oxygen, even as it sucks up the last his body has to give. Grown far too large, his mind pops like a balloon, and there is no more pain, only floating freely, and in this numb state he finds what he's been looking for all these years.

Light returns, first as stars, his brain cells exploding one after the other, setting off a fireworks display across the blank void of his sight. Then it is a great, giant orb, glowing white and growing each second, expanding to fill his vision as it rushes at him, or he at it. It swallows him just as he is ready to let go of life.

Lost in blissful release, he lets it engulf him. But it is not a mouth which consumes him. Nor is this light heaven, taking in his weary soul. It is a hole, with the sun shining beyond. He passes out of it, a great torrent of water spitting his battered body back into the world. The earth itself rejects him as it vomits him out with the other detritus it dredges up from its bowels, dumping the sick mixture upon the tundra—rocks, dinosaurs, and people, the dead and the living alike, strewn across the snow.

24

For long moments, Roman believes he is dead. Then the pain returns and he knows he is not. It is hardly a relief or a comfort to still be alive; the hard, cold bite of the tundra is a sharp reminder of the price which comes with life. The pain spreads through his body in the form of rigor mortis stiffness, his limbs only groggily remembering how to move, and when they do, the agony in the joints is like the snapping of twigs, his skin shattered glass he rolls upon. All the bumps and scrapes he suffered, hurtling through the tunnel like so much flotsam and jetsam, flare like the searing scalds of boiling water. He hisses, the steam floating free of his mouth, his body still hot, but cooling quickly now he's on the surface. More vapour rises from his wet clothes, sucking further heat out of him. Already the moisture there is freezing, a fragile crust of thin ice which crackles as he sits up and looks about.

His jaw drops at the sight. All is destruction and chaos.

There is water everywhere, its surface sparkling in the sunshine and cut through with the taint of fresh blood. Already it is seeping into the snow and ice, becoming one with it, freezing despite the sun's pale rays. A brisk breeze ripples the bloodied water, cooling it further and sculpting it into tiny frozen waves of crystalline ruby. The wind cuts straight through Roman, chilling him to the bone. But this isn't why a shiver tingles down his spine.

It's the bodies. Not human, but dinosaur; so many, and of every type imaginable. Most are dead, carved and pulverised mountains of destroyed flesh, their gory entrails strewn far and wide by the explosive force of the water expelled through the cave's mouth. Others cling to life, if only barely. They flop like fish out of water, their mouths groping for air. Some fight to stand, yet collapse under their own weight, with broken limbs, or simply weakened from too long locked in the ice.

The most grievously injured remain still, ready to die, or longing to return to the embrace of the ice. As the wind freezes the water which coats them, they will not have to wait long to be entombed once more. A few are not so keen on such a fate, hauling themselves up and wandering off into the depths of the tundra, where the same result awaits, simply delayed. Roman feels this fate clawing at him as well. Death seems certain.

"No," he tells himself, prising apart lips which are frozen together. They sting with windburn already. This pain seems more intense than all the other dull aches which plague his whole frame, and it steels him, reminding him he's alive. While he feels this pain, he still has a chance. It is the slow, creeping numbness he must fear most now, that which nearly stole him away in the depths of the water. That blissful escape is nothing more than an illusion, tempting him to embrace the death he has so sorely sought.

And which he now rejects utterly.

He takes a deep breath in, cherishes the cool freshness, ignoring the bitter tang of blood which sticks in the back of his throat. It gathers there likc a stagnant pool, seeking to pollute him. He hawks it up and spits it out, leaves it on the tundra.

With no small amount of effort, he lifts himself up out of the icy blood and gore. In the distance are the mountains, fresh and white, yet changed from before, lesser, a layer of their pale skin torn away by the searing heat of the sun and the molten rock beneath the turbulent Earth's crust. The pass there is a deep V-shaped gouge, carved as if by the strike of a godly axe, no longer filled to the brim with snow.

He longs to venture there, to see what is beyond. What fresh life might be waiting for him past this previously impassable boundary? But this dream is crushed by a single word, spoken by a gravelly voice like an invocation which binds him to this realm of cold and pain.

"Roman," it says.

Roman turns and spits back the name of the speaker like a reciprocal word of power, trying to banish them.

"Trent."

It is no spectre or demon Roman looks at, but a man, fragile and vulnerable, and so they persist instead of fading into the dazzling mirage light of the tundra. If this is a disappointment to Roman, he has at least some solace in the form of his tormentor's suffering.

Trent looks like he's been pulled from a watery grave, sodden through, his face pinched with pain, lips tinged with blue and his beard sparkling with dangling icicles. His body sags under the gravity of grave wounds, as well as the backpack he carries as if it contains all he has in the world, which indeed it might. He has a broken arm, the bone protruding through his jacket, and his good hand trembles as he cradles this terrible injury.

Roman smiles to see it, the least of what the man deserves, but as his eyes scan downwards, he finds the jagged hunk of metal which juts from Trent's abdomen. His smile drops. Even schadenfreude has its limits.

"You're alive," says Trent, as if he can't believe it, can't believe he himself is still breathing. Roman isn't sure how long this can be said for either of them. They're both shivering so much they vibrate.

"We need to get you back to the base," says Roman, not believing he's saying it.

"Your blood?" says Trent, his voice stretched thin by pain, making the question sound like the plea of a desperate vampire on the brink of second death.

Roman offers his upturned hands, empty. "I lost it in the flood."

"That damn Brock," hisses Trent, wincing with pain as anger tenses his body. "He just had to go back for you."

"If he didn't, I'd be dead, and the blood would be gone all the same."

"Damn it, Roman. Don't you get it yet? I *need* that blood to bribe people, *powerful* people, or they'll rain hell on all our heads."

"I think it's a bit late for that," says Roman, eyeing the devastation which surrounds them, the piles of dinosaur carcasses. He sees no dark green scales mottled with red among the dead, and concern gnaws at his guts. He sees no sign of Brock, either, and is surprised by the sadness which darkens his mind.

"You need to find it," says Trent. "The backpack has to be here somewhere."

"You do it. I'm heading back before I freeze."

"Over my dead body."

"Might be exactly what I step over, the state you're in."

Trent straightens with effort. His body shudders, and not with the cold. "I'm not done yet."

"I might have lost the blood in the deluge, but looks like you lost your gun, too."

"You need the blood just as much as I do," says Trent. He jerks his head over his shoulder at the pack on his back. "This will buy us only so much time."

"I don't need shit from you." Roman turns his back and scans about. Estimating where they'd left the snowmobiles, he strides in that direction, skirting around a hill of dead dinosaurs and passing by the yawning mouth of the cave, partially clogged with debris. Water laps at its bottom edge, the whole underground system filled up with the stuff.

"Please," says a small voice filled with pain.

Roman stops, not believing what he's hearing. Is Trent actually begging for his help?

"Please help me."

Roman slowly turns. Movement catches in the periphery of his sight and he locks onto it. A pathetic figure drags itself through the detritus of rock and snow at the cave's mouth. Roman gasps with shock.

Brock is still alive.

25

Roman rushes to his side. Brock's body is a shattered wreck; he doesn't so much crawl as paw desperately at anything within reach. Roman holds out a hand and Brock grasps it, the grip slipping in the wet.

"Hold on, mate, we're getting you out," says Roman.

"We don't have time for this," says Trent, coming up behind, wheezing with strain.

"He came back for me. I have to help him," says Roman, but as he splashes in the water to get a better hold, more of Brock's horrific injuries are revealed. It seems hopeless. His lower body is crushed, wrinkled and flat as a squeezed-out tube of toothpaste. He makes a terrible strangled sound, mewling like a wounded animal as Roman tries to pull him clear of the debris.

"He's stuck, leave him," says Trent, standing over Brock. Brock looks up at him, teeth clenched with hate and agony. He tries to speak, but the words are nothing but a gasping spray of spittle.

"I'll fucking leave you before I'm leaving him," says Roman, bitter tears stinging his skin as they freeze on his cheeks. He can see Trent is right. Brock's foot is caught under a chunk of ice the size of a boulder. He grabs Brock's leg to give it a desperate pull, but as he does so the leg itself stretches with a sick sound of shredded muscle and a crackle of shattered bone. Brock screams, a high shriek which descends through a torturous octave of suffering to settle into a pitiful wail which persists even after Roman stops. The foot isn't budging.

"We'll go back to the base and get help," says Trent, seeing Roman isn't giving up despite the obvious hopelessness of the situation.

"He'll be dead by the time we get back," says Roman, eyes darting over the rocks and ice, trying to figure out a way to free the foot.

"I'll die if we don't go now."

Roman grunts as he shifts a rock. "Good."

"If I had my gun—"

Roman straightens, getting in Trent's face. "You'd what, shoot me? And what good would that do? Who would drive you back to base? Who would harvest your precious blood?"

"I was going to say, to put him out of his misery."

Brock's eyes roll like billiard balls under bright lights. Trent doesn't meet their tumbling gaze.

"Oh, now you're done with him, he can be cast aside, is that it? You can't solve all your problems with the barrel of a gun, you know!" shouts Roman, driving Trent back a step. Frantic, Roman returns to trying to free Brock. His failing strength struggles to lift each mossy rock, slick with blood. He's kidding himself, moving only those around the big chunk of ice, which is too heavy to budge.

"He's a killer. Don't forget that," Trent says coldly.

"He's what *you* made him, what this *fucking place* made him." Roman is spitting with fury. He kicks a large rock. It shifts and turns unnaturally, sliding across the other rocks beneath with an ominous grating.

"I'm a victim of this base as well," says Trent, real feeling in his voice. "I want my freedom. I want to see my daughter again."

"So, it doesn't matter who else dies along the way, as long as you get out?" asks Roman, a trembling finger pointed at Trent.

Trent doesn't answer. He's frowning down at the rock Roman kicked and slowly backing away as if afraid to trigger an avalanche. Brock has his mad eyes locked on the same spot. Roman turns slowly, afraid of what he'll see.

The rock is no longer sliding over the others. There is silence except for the howling wind, a delicate balance maintained, but only for the moment. Roman leans in to look at the rock. It is mossy green, like the others, but the texture is different, not fuzzy.

"It's *scaly*," he says, and the red splotches are not blood at all.

The surface of the rock splits open to reveal a staring, reptilian eye.

"Holy fuck!"

Roman jumps back, his body spring-loaded as a jolt of electric terror surges through him. Brock writhes impotently on the ground, unable to escape as Trent hobbles away as fast as he can. Roman maintains his distance but doesn't follow, watching in horror as a translucent, nictitating membrane blinks across the surface of the slitted eye.

The rock is not a rock at all. It is the head of the Tyrannosaurus rex.

The massive monster lies prone, half buried under debris in the mouth of the cave. It huffs through a puckering nostril like the scaly anus of a crocodile, clearing its breathing passage of grit. Both Roman and Brock hear this for the warning it is, and go completely still, praying the eye can't see them if they don't move. But the vertical black slit shifts back and forth between the two of them. The Tyrannosaurus's jaw cracks open as if with a devilish grin, revealing huge, off-white teeth.

Conical, yet sharp and slightly serrated; perfect for rending flesh. Brock sees these grisly tools, so close to his face and he shrieks like a boiling kettle.

Roman turns and runs across bloody snow. He doesn't need to see what comes next, though he can hear it even if he doesn't want that either. With a grinding sound like the beginning of a rockslide, the Tyrannosaurus shifts its bulk. Brock's screaming rises in pitch, a piercing wail of mortal terror. It is abruptly silenced with a sick crunch of cracking ribs followed by a popping burst of spilling gore.

There are more sounds of heavy rocks shifting and tumbling as the Tyrannosaurus fights its way free of the rubble, and then Roman's guts turn to jelly as the air is rent by a mighty roar of feasting triumph. Reality seems to waver with passing shockwaves. Roman feels dizzy, the colossal noise punching deep into his eardrums, nearly throwing him off-balance.

It takes everything he has to stay on his feet, to keep running, afraid the Tyrannosaurus is chasing him. He hears massive booms and is certain they are the huge footfalls of the monster giving chase. But it is just his heart, loud in his ringing ears.

The sense of looming dread doesn't leave him even as he reaches the snowmobile, where Trent stands, bent double, attempting to both clutch his broken arm and put pressure on his stomach at once. He still wears the backpack as if it's the only thing keeping him afloat in a violent sea of suffering.

"What are you waiting for?" Roman screams at him. Trent is too weak to reply, and just barely manages to lift his head and give him a withering glare, its meaning clear: he's in no state to drive, only waiting for Roman because he needs him.

Roman scowls and stomps past Trent, furious with him, but even more so with himself for leaving Brock. It helps not at all to know there was nothing he could do to save him, or the fact that, without Brock as a distraction, he'd be in the jaws of the Tyrannosaurus himself right now.

Neither is a solace for the burning sting of his own cowardice, giving in to self-preservation rather than doing what is right. Brock fought against that feeling, coming back for Roman in the cave. Given the same choice, Roman ran, and is still running, aware the dinosaur will soon be coming for him, too.

There is only one snowmobile, the second flattened by the falling weight of a dinosaur carcass shot from the cave mouth by the explosive water pressure. He mounts up, applies the choke, and hits the electric starter, praying the motor will kick in. It rumbles for a moment and conks out.

"Fuck!" says Roman. He's not sure the pounding he hears now is still his heart. The dinosaur is searching for them among the mounds of carcasses.

"Push the kill switch up to the run position," says Trent through gritted teeth. Roman curses himself out as Trent awkwardly throws his leg over the seat and sinks down gingerly, hissing in Roman's ear the whole time. Roman grimaces and strongly considers barging Trent off the back. But maybe he's right. Maybe they need his contacts and the blood on his back to survive the winter.

The ground shakes. The Tyrannosaurus is coming. Roman doesn't look back. He pushes the kill switch to run, hits the starter, and the snowmobile comes to life with a tinny whine of its revving engine. Feeling death bearing down on him, an avalanche of flesh and teeth about to fall, Roman accelerates, leaving the Tyrannosaurus in his wake, not looking back.

26

There's smoke rising on the horizon, an ugly smudge of black marring the infinite blue sky. There is a similar dark cloud filling Roman's mind, dense as guilt. He'd never liked Brock, never had reason to—until he saved Roman's life. The fact he could have returned that favour—and in doing so, given his own life meaning—but instead ran, saving himself yet losing his humanity, is too much to bear. It weighs him down like exhaustion, and he barely has the strength to keep his grip on the accelerator, to keep moving forward. He has no choice but to continue despite his weariness. The dark cloud looms, spreading from his thoughts to taint the perfect white of the tundra, billowing from its source, both inside and outside of himself.

His whole world is on fire.

There's nothing he can do but go towards the flames. They sparkle translucently on the horizon and burn inside his body, and he can't tell which of these—if either—are phantom sensations. The withdrawals from the gummies are finally catching up with him proper. He feels freezing cold at his core, but his skin tingles as his body furiously dumps the last of its heat into the atmosphere. There are gusts of warmth radiating across the tundra as well, meaning the fire in the distance must be real, despite its cause being concealed by the dark smear of smoke spreading like a storm front.

Unpleasant smells wafting on the breeze hold clues. Seared charcoal, combusting petroleum, and the carcinogenic chemical reek of burning asbestos. Roman's nostrils itch with the taint of it. He snuffles to clear the stench, but it lingers, telling a story of events hidden by the smoke. It hangs in the air like amnesia, obscuring painful events from the past.

Roman slows the snowmobile to a sputtering crawl as he teases the edges of this artificial cloud bank, the sooty air hanging dense near the ground, leaden with heavy metal tang. But there's something in the olfactory mix which makes him even more wary. A sickly-sweet note strikes the back of his throat, making him gag.

It's burning flesh.

"Huh? What?" says Trent, snuffling himself awake with a snort. He'd been nodding in and out the whole trip, his pain mercifully pulling him away from consciousness only to torturously drag him back again. Now the smoke acts like smelling salts and he coughs loudly in Roman's ear.

Roman's own throat tickles, but he suppresses it, desperate to hear any clues of what's happening around him in this fog of war. He has little hope, however, Trent's curses alternating with disgusting gagging.

"Oh, my fucking God, that hurts," says Trent, spluttering warm moisture onto Roman's check. Roman lifts his glove, the fingers frozen stiff. He touches his face, also frozen, and wipes the moisture away. He looks at the frosted fingertips of his gloves, glistening with rubies.

Blood.

"You're dying," he says, his voice as cold and flat as the tundra.

"I fucking know that," says Trent, fighting to suppress his coughing, clutching his one good hand against his rebellious diaphragm, the shuddering movement aggravating the horrendous puncture wound in his gut. He coughs more blood onto the back of Roman's hood. "Get me to the base."

Roman double checks the GPS. "We're there."

"What?" says Trent in hushed wonder, looking around at the smoke as if seeing it for the first time. Flames flicker through its opaque barrier like distant stars. The heat melts the frosty layer covering both men, steam making them soggy but failing to warm their cores after too long spent wet in the bitter wind.

"It's on fire," says Roman, nudging the snowmobile forward until the familiar boxy silhouette of the base appears in the murk, crowned with a halo of flames.

***

The main building isn't the only thing on fire. Flickering silhouettes dart about in the hazy pall of smoke, arms flailing. Human torches set ablaze by the raging inferno, their screams speak of impossible pain no one should have to bear. Some collapse in the snow in feeble attempts to quell the flames, shrieking as they roll, yet each falling silent as the fire steals their oxygen and consumes their flesh. Others keep running, as if fleeing an even more horrible fate, their pitiful wails of panicked terror piercing Roman's frosty armour, making him sag under the dripping weight of melting ice flowing off his body.

"I don't understand," gasps Trent, incomprehension momentarily winning out over his agony. "What's happened?"

"What do you think happened? *You* happened."

"Me?"

"You and your doomed fucking rebellion. Did you think *they* were going to take this lying down? The sadistic fucks who imprisoned us here and kill anyone who gets close enough to discover the truth? They bombed us, just like they bombed that damned boat that came nosing around!"

Trent's fingers scrape at Roman's back, the claws of a desperate, cornered beast. "B-but… but I have the blood!"

"It's too late for that. Perhaps it always was. Do you really think they would have bartered with you for our lives? For our freedom?"

"My contact—"

"Was on the resupply ship, yes?"

Trent's fingers dig into Roman's shoulder as he grasps the depth of his error.

Roman shucks off the man's tight hold. "And when they couldn't get in to take possession of the blood," he continues, "they freaked out, because all hell was breaking loose, what with your little enterprise and the coast cracking apart."

"I can still save us," pleads Trent.

"Save who? Look around you. Everyone's dead, or soon to be, including us, if we don't do something."

Roman isn't sure what this something is, so he lets the snowmobile idle, not knowing where to turn in the swirling maelstrom of smoke and fire. They can't stay here, and yet to flee blindly into the tundra is to die a slow death of hypothermia and starvation.

"You, me… *we* can survive!" says Trent, clutching Roman around the waist and holding him tight.

Roman grimaces as the smoke closes in around them, seeming to cut them off from the rest of the world. He hates that his fate is tied to Trent, not wanting anything to do with him. Once more he thinks of leaving him to die, but he has no plan of his own, so he lets Trent cling to him, as much as it disgusts him.

"How?" he asks. "And this better be good."

"I have a stash," Trent whispers in Roman's ear conspiratorially. Roman hears the word stash and he perks up, the promise of relief from this nightmare dangling before him.

"You have gummies somewhere?" he asks, hardly believing an escape hatch is being offered to him, a way out of the blinding, choking smoke and into a blissful haze of light.

"Not gummies," growls Trent indignantly. "The fuck we going to do with gummies now?"

"I just want out of here," says Roman sincerely, breathy as a prayer. A gap in the smoke opens like a doorway. He turns towards this portal, light shining beyond.

Through it runs a person. Though not on fire, they wave their arms and scream frantic nonsense, eyes wild with terror. Their cries are cut short as a dark shape pounces. It bursts through the dense wall of cloying smog in their wake, flattening them into the snow with a dull thump.

Roman can't believe what he's seeing. A creature perches atop the stricken man, pressing down with its weight and driving the long talons of its hind feet into their neck. The claws work like butcher's knives, slicing open flesh in long downwards strokes, exposing the spine. Blood splashes in a hot jet across the snow as the creature looks up from its kill, the eye on the side of its long face meeting Roman's.

It's a velociraptor.

27

Survival-induced terror signals light up in Roman's brain, but his body is sluggish to respond, his adrenal glands long since squeezed dry by prolonged exposure to sources of mortal threat. Luckily, the velociraptor isn't in a hurry either, content with its kill and happy to bury its snout in the warm gore of the man's exposed insides.

Roman guns the engine of the snowmobile, a high revving whine which sounds like a snarl. *Too much* like a snarl. Another velociraptor lunges from the opposite side while Roman is distracted. It would have barrelled into him, knocking him from his seat, but he sends the vehicle forward, and the leaping predator instead lands on the first dinosaur, sending both tumbling. Roman accelerates, leaving them hissing and snarling at each other as they bicker over the dead lump of meat in the snow.

***

Exiting the roiling banks of smoke, Roman enters another maelstrom, one of death and violence. Zooming left and right, he pushes the snowmobile to the limit, running the gauntlet of frenzied velociraptors which seem to press in from all sides. They chirp with excitement, calling on each other to work together to corner the fresh meat.

Time and again, Roman barely manages to squeeze between the pincer charge of a pair of dinosaurs, coming at him from both flanks at once. They pass in front and behind him, arcing through the air, claws to the fore as they leap to knock him from his perch. Trent, barely holding on with fading strength, is nearly toppled from the snowmobile by Roman's frantic manoeuvrings. It would be so easy to turn hard and skid, throwing him off the back, giving Roman precious time to escape while the dinosaurs feast on his flesh. But he doesn't. Loathe as he is to admit it, he still needs Trent.

"Where am I going?" Roman shouts over the wind of the speeding vehicle and the omnipresent snarling of hungry predators closing in.

"That way," says Trent, his voice barely audible. His hand, clutching Roman's shoulder, points with a single quivering finger.

Roman shifts the handlebars. It aims them directly at a velociraptor. Rather than steer around or slow down, he revs the snowmobile and ploughs into the dinosaur as it's turning. It goes down with a shrill squeal of agony and a thump which jolts the vehicle as if taking a speedbump far too fast. Trent sways and nearly topples over. Roman reaches back with a hand to catch him, holding him steady.

"I need more than some vague direction," says Roman. "Give me some GPS co-ordinates."

"I don't have any," Trent wheezes with the effort of staying upright. "I just use landmarks."

It sounds like a lie, and Roman is sure it is. Trent is anything but stupid. He's holding tight to his last bargaining chip.

"Landmarks?" says Roman, trying to force the issue by pointing out the obvious flaw in the argument. To him, the tundra looks infinite, a plain of featureless ice and snow broken only in the distance by the black spear tips of the mountains.

"I've been here…" says Trent, fading further with each word. He takes his time, and many shallow breaths, before finishing his sentence. "A lot longer than you."

"And what?" asks Roman. "You stashed supplies against the day you'd finally make your run for it? Some type of bugout bag as insurance against catastrophe?"

Without the strength to say more, Trent squeezes Roman's shoulder as confirmation.

"Okay, then," says Roman with a resigned sigh. "Which way now?"

Trent points, and Roman adjusts his steering. They speed off into the endless tundra, trailing a horde of hungry velociraptors.

28

Fortunately for both Roman and Trent, the velociraptors give up the chase before the snowmobile runs out of petrol. There's easier prey, in the form of injured stegosauruses, to be found on the tundra, and one by one, the velociraptors peel off to follow these lumbering hunks of near-dead meat, rather than trying to keep pace with a speeding vehicle promising a less abundant meal.

"We're mostly gristle anyway," says Roman, laughing at his own joke when Trent doesn't. His laughter dies away as the snowmobile's engine splutters. It struggles on for a few more seconds in jerky spurts and then conks out with a cough of fumes from its exhaust. They slide to a halt.

"I guess the joke's on us after all," says Roman, dismounting. As he does, Trent topples from the seat, landing with a crunch in powdery snow. Roman crouches next to him, gives his shoulder a shake. "Trent?"

The man wheezes. Blood soaks his clothes around his abdomen, frozen into icicles like a glistening, crystalline scab. The cold temperature is the only reason he hasn't already bled out.

"Hey, Trent. We're out of fuel. Please tell me there's petrol in this cache of yours."

No answer.

"Which way? We've got to be close, right?"

Trent doesn't point, unable to lift his arm. He merely shifts his head slightly and stares mutely.

"Over there?" Roman gets low to look along Trent's line of sight. "What am I looking for?"

Trent's lips curl with the effort of forcing them apart. Roman holds his ear to them to catch the single word.

"Landmark," Trent says with a faint, mirthless chuckle like air escaping a corpse.

Roman frowns and lifts his head. He looks in the direction indicated and sees nothing but more whiteness.

"The fuck?" he says, getting up. Sick of this shit, but with nothing else to pin his hopes upon, he starts walking, trudging through freshly fallen snow. It's a slog, but he keeps going, eyes fixed forward, seeing nothing.

He stops and looks back at Trent, who is an unmoving lump sprinkled with snow. He might as well be a corpse. Roman throws his hands up in frustration and looks around for something, anything. Finding nothing, he heads off-course, taking a dozen steps to the side. Looking back the way Trent had indicated now, there's a subtle change in the quality of the infinite whiteness, as if some type of depth has been added; the vaguest of shadows, a less pure white.

Heading towards this, it disappears. Roman slaps his flanks in frustration. But then he takes a few steps to the side, and a few more, until the shadow returns. He repeats this, going forward and to the side until the landscape resolves into a shape. More precisely, a mound.

Buried beneath the snow, it is white on white, and it seems to pop into existence only when Roman is basically on top of it. How Trent could see it from a distance, much less navigate to it, is beyond him. Although, when life is on the line, strange and fantastic things are possible; Roman's own survival proof enough of that, a surprise to himself as much as anyone.

He looks around for some type of explanation for Trent's miraculous feat of fieldcraft, and his eyes settle on the mountains. The much larger cousins of the mound he stands before, they're enough of a landmark to navigate by; their peaks are a distinct zigzag pattern on the horizon, some taller than others, like points on a compass. Roman sees the pass with its young river of meltwater he saw earlier, its location as locked as true north, although he knows it is to the south of the base. All the mountains are.

"You're a resourceful bastard, I'll give you that," Roman says of Trent, a sentiment he has cause to repeat as he unearths the cache. He has to first scrape away the thick snow and crack through a brittle layer of ice with annoyed stomps of his cleated boots, but then it is all gravy as he hauls out a sled covered in a rubber tarp. It crackles with frost as he pulls it back to reveal the glorious gifts of Trent's bounty.

Ration packs, tins of water, extreme weather clothing, a tent, sleeping bags, a flashlight, flare gun, waterproof matches, and a gas stove; everything a man needs to survive in the harsh wilderness of the tundra, at least for a while. It might not be everything, but it's enough.

It is life itself.

Most importantly, there are two jerry cans of petrol for the snowmobile. Roman picks these up, giving them a slosh, relieved they aren't frozen. Forget the blood. This is the liquid which will save them, and he'll have to think hard about how to make best use of it. Where can they turn for safety?

For now, though, he's not going anywhere. Completely spent, he barely has the energy to pitch the tent, strip himself and Trent of their sodden, frost-rimed clothing, and stuff them both into sleeping bags before he falls into the welcoming arms of unconsciousness.

***

Roman awakes from a sleep so deep he thought he was dead. He returns to the land of the living, greeted by the tingling pain of biting cold, penetrating even the thick, thermal layers of the sleeping bag. He reaches out and touches the inside of the tent. The surface is as cold as ice. He reaches in the opposite direction to touch Trent's forehead. It is just as cold.

Roman takes a slow, deep breath in and out. There is no panic. No frantic rush to action. He already knows.

Trent's eyes are closed. He could be sleeping. But he isn't.

He's dead.

29

Roman lies on his back and stares at the tent's ceiling for a long time. Outside, the wind howls like a wild beast, shaking the tent as if trying to spook him. But he is beyond feeling anything. Anything, except perhaps loneliness. It returns like an unwelcome guest to reside in his head, taking up too much space, his thoughts no company at all, expressing not even negative sentiments. He is left with nothing but a yawning void, inside and out, all alone on the infinite tundra.

He can't even bring himself to care that there are no gummies, no means of escape, even for a little while. Not even the small death of sleep has refreshed him, merely made it possible for his body to function at all, which it does so automatically, with no conscious volition from him, wriggling out of the sleeping bag and reaching for fresh clothes. The air is freezing as he moves from one soft, warm cocoon to the other, stirring him a little through the discomfort, reminding him of the suffering which is waiting for him outside the tent.

Wrapped up as best he can in a new set of clothes, it's easy to forget what awaits him out there, until, of course, he looks down at Trent's pale face tinged with blue. Even with the eyes closed it seems to stare at him in accusation, not peaceful at all, but full of worry, the brow a maze of deep creases, like he's carried all his cares into the next life with him. It's not reassuring for Roman, to know that not even the dead rest in peace.

He reaches down and pulls the zipper of Trent's sleeping bag all the way up over his head. This doesn't make Roman feel any better, only hides the problem, so he drags the bag outside. He doesn't have burial in mind, but neither is it necessary. Snow falls on the sleeping bag, with the dark lump of humanity slowly being covered by the pure white of the tundra. Sadness eludes Roman. He never cared for Trent. But he was someone to talk to, and Roman feels that loss, if not for the actual person Trent was.

Thinking it only right to say some solemn words, Roman realises he doesn't really know this man at all. Years on a base together and yet there's nothing to be said. Roman sees his own reflection in this lack, an indictment of his personal failure. Imprisoned against his will at the base, he isolated himself even more than the situation demanded, retreating into himself to escape. In the process he lost his chance at forming relationships with the few humans left in his life—his fellow prisoners—all dead now, connection impossible. All that remains are memories and missed opportunities, tenuous links to the past best cut.

"I'm sorry for your daughter," he says finally, the family tie the only nugget in Trent's life that Roman can grasp on to. It seems a worthless sentiment. Most likely the daughter already thought Trent died years ago. What difference does today make? None, except to Trent himself, and what does that matter now, his life over, and the only person to mark its passing knowing nothing of him?

It seems a brutal fate. One which awaits Roman too. No, his death will be worse, because there will be no one there.

"If a tree falls in the woods…" he says and feels a tug at his heartstrings with this sentiment. His own family won't even know he's gone, not for sure. They'll live in limbo, hope mingled with despair until, finally, they die, too.

Perhaps they're already dead? Roman finds himself wishing this is so, a small mercy to save them from the suffering of not knowing what became of him. Or maybe they've already given him up for dead and moved on? This is the worst fate of all. To not be loved enough to be remembered. This seems impossible, yet, with a flash of guilt, Roman finds he can't quite picture his parents' faces.

He frowns, squeezing his mind with the effort, but their features are nothing more than hazy guesses conjured up like smoke, dissipating and distorting further with time. The longer he spends away from home, the worse it will get, until they are nothing at all, and he nothing to them, either.

This fact finally brings a tear to his eye. It tumbles down his cheek and dangles from his chin, freezing into a perfect crystalline gem, before falling, lost with the rest of the snowflakes. Unique, yet lost in the masses.

30

By the time Roman sets up the gas stove before the tent's flaps, melting a handful of snow to brew some coffee, Trent is gone, covered by the snow. Alone again, he tries not to think about what's waiting for him out there on the tundra. He hears roaring, and whether it's the Tyrannosaurus, or the raging fire of the base consumed by further bombs, is unclear. The sound echoes off the mountains so it's impossible to tell its direction, seeming to come from all of them at once, squeezing Roman between a rock and a hard place.

***

With the hot coffee warming his guts, and some rations thoughtlessly and haphazardly thrown on top, Roman feels a little better, human even. The snow continues to fall, burying all his sins beneath a uniform layer of white powder. It is a blessed relief. He knows he could have done more to help Trent, but that's in the past. Whether he purposefully let him bleed out, or was merely too exhausted to care, is no longer relevant. Trent is just another frozen body in the ground, like the dinosaurs. Though, unlike them, he won't be coming back. For this, Roman is thankful.

He's also thankful for the sled of supplies, which he dutifully packs up and hooks onto the back of the snowmobile. He pours a rationed portion of petrol into the gas tank and places the pack of blood upon his back. The stuff is still worth money, if he ever gets out of here. He's surprised he can even countenance such a possibility, and this gives him hope, even if it is delusional.

Climbing astride the seat of the snowmobile he feels like a new man, a cowboy in the saddle embarking on an adventure upon an unknown frontier. There's no one left who remembers the old him, not even himself, and he vows to forget the gummies, forget death. Both were always just a means to escape living; one temporary, the other permanent.

For better or worse, he is now in charge of his own destiny, no longer goaded by the will of others or imprisoned by circumstance.

It is a dizzying sensation, existential vertigo nearly sending him tumbling from his seat. He grips the handlebars for support, finds them comfortingly solid, aware he can give them direction. Perhaps, if he's lucky and resourceful enough, he'll survive.

Filled with a new vigour for life, and a burning desire to at least try to make something out of this shitshow, he starts the engine. The only problem is that, as he stares into the obscuring blizzard of snow, he has no idea which way to go.

***

Roman looks ahead. The semi-obscured sun is a dull smear, its light defused across a haze of white, the snowstorm a moving fuzz of blurred static. In the other direction is a dirty darkness of shifting greys and browns, the light gobbled up by the storm, inhabited only by the wind. Its rising shrieks sound like the panicked cries of pursued prey, followed afterwards by those of the hunters, the wind swooping low into the long howls of hungry beasts hot on the trail.

A shudder runs down Roman's spine, not wanting to plunge into the terrible unknown of the turbulent dark. He favours the light. Not used to making his own choices, he trusts it to guide him, even if it is a false promise and neither forward nor back promises safety. He'd be groping blind regardless, the sun useless both for direction and sight.

With no visual clues to go by, he has no choice but to trust himself and what he knows. He scrapes a dense layer of snow from the screen of the GPS using his glove and leans close to peer at the screen. Its faint glow provides only the most basic of information, not much more than a standard compass. He's never been this far out into the tundra, so his coordinates mean nothing besides placing him somewhere to the south of the base and north of the mountains. Beyond this vague location, he may as well be in a featureless field of white—because that's exactly where he is. It stretches infinitely to the east and west, the tundra a ring girdling the entire continent.

Roman frowns in consternation. Annoyed that his choice is dictated more by what he *cannot* do than his own preferences, he starts ruling out possibilities.

He has no intention of heading north. He'll find no refuge in the rubble of the destroyed base, and the people who destroyed it could still be watching, ready to pick off survivors. Besides, the coast there is a riven wreck of shattered icebergs, with no ships able to come to his rescue. Even if they did, he might find them less than welcoming. He hasn't come all this way to simply catch a bullet.

East or west, then? The two seem interchangeable; he has no knowledge of what lies in either direction. He'd be flipping a coin as to which is best. If he got it right, he might find his way to some safe harbour while skirting close to the coast, or signal a friendly ship with a flare, but if he got it wrong…

The thought of pushing on blindly into an endless expanse—no one for hundreds or thousands of kilometres, his fuel and food running out—is too much to bear. He flings it from his mind, even as he realises it's the most likely outcome no matter which way he goes.

And there is only one option left.

South.

To the mountains.

***

Trent and Brock came over the mountains, however involuntarily. The American base lies somewhere in that direction, and while it did them no favours in the end—they were drugged and human trafficked in coffins—Roman convinces himself that it won't be the same for him. There's no way to know if the whole base is rotten or merely contains corrupt elements. Perhaps it's best that this is so, because it implies the presence of an amoral black market. If there's any chance, any chance at all, that he can trade the blood on his back for passage on a ship, he has to take it. It's his only shot, and a long one at that.

But he has to try.

31

The disembodied ghosts of the wind and the tinny revving of the snowmobile are Roman's only companions as he pushes on into the blizzard, guided by the bearing on the GPS screen. He keeps it locked on due south, ignoring his foreboding as the smudge of the sun rotates around him, plunging him into periods of obscuring darkness alternating with blinding light.

Occasionally, he's forced to stop, pouring fuel into the gas tank and emptying his bladder, but otherwise he has no choice but to push on, hoping for the best. If the mountains are too far away, he's doomed. But if he can just reach them…

He slowly brings the snowmobile to a halt. He leans on the vibrating handlebars of the idling vehicle, staring thoughtfully into the blizzard, which is finally starting to ease a little.

Reach the mountains, and then what? The snowmobile can only take him so far. Afterwards, he's on foot, his only supplies what he can carry. Will he ditch the blood to carry more food? If he does that, what will he use to barter? His mind flickers through combinations of what to take with him and what he can afford to leave, a balance sheet of trade-offs he cannot make work. Each piece of equipment seems vital to survival, every bite of food more strength to continue. He needs more time to find an answer, but he doesn't have time.

Glimpsed through the thinning snowfall, he sees the jagged outline of a row of peaks.

***

The zigzag battlements of the mountain range waver like a mirage in the slanting streams of falling snow, disappearing one moment, reappearing the next, a promise of shelter held always at arm's length, growing no larger as Roman zooms towards them.

He checks his bearing. He's drifted from due south, but this shouldn't be the case. All the mountains are to the south. Slowing to a crawl, he waits until the snow clears enough that he can get a visual reference point. He locks onto and drives towards the tallest mountain he can see, its single spiked point flanked by a fanning arc of peaks mounted upon a ridge. But even this static reference point seems to shift, the bearing sliding from true like the gaze of a lazy eye.

"What in the hell?" says Roman, disconcerted to be turning the handlebars further to keep himself pointed at this distinctive formation of peaks.

Then something even weirder happens.

Another rock formation appears as if by magic, not from beyond the snow, but as if pushing *through* it. It is a giant, humpbacked mountain, long and low, with an undulating dip rising across a ridge to a knotted knoll at one end. Dark and foreboding, the whole mass trembles as if shaken by an earthquake. In an impossible move, it picks itself up and shifts a few degrees across the horizon.

Roman stiffens in alarm, and blinks rapidly, unsure if his eyes are deceiving him in the blizzard. He keeps going, his curiosity overwhelming him as he sees the fanning mountain range seem to react to this movement, itself jolting to one side as if in fright.

"Is this something to do with that geothermal event Trent mentioned?" Roman asks himself. "Perhaps tectonic plates grinding against one another?"

He hears strange sounds carried on the strong winds of the blizzard, and they very well could be the rumbling of tectonic plates deep in the ground, their movements shifting mountains on the surface like the lunge and clash of colossal weapons of stone.

But as Roman moves towards this seismic event, the sound crashes over him, far closer and louder than he could have imagined. For a second, he believes the frosty ground beneath his vehicle is going to split open and swallow him whole. But the rumbling rises to a roar, and it is not the roar of sundered earth.

It is the roar of an enraged beast.

32

Roman realises far too late that the mountains are not mountains at all. They pivot on the spot and move towards him—an impossible feat even for an earthquake. Not far away and hugely massive at all, but instead much closer and simply large, they turn into the grain of the blizzard and become clearly visible for the first time. Roman feels a tremorous quake of terror ripple through his guts to see the monsters revealed.

Dinosaurs.

The arched fan of mountain peaks is really the splay of bony plates upon the back of a stegosaurus. Lumbering straight at Roman at full gallop, the bulky creature bleats and honks in panicked fear as it flees its pursuer, that which Roman had mistaken for the undulating mountain.

Far more terrifying than even the unstoppable bulk of a charging five tonne stegosaurus, it is a Tyrannosaurus rex. It is *the* Tyrannosaurus rex, its distinctive mossy green scales mottled with red as if splashed with gore. It opens its huge jaws, teeth like bone swords glinting, speckled with old blood. The apex predator emits a monstrous roar, momentarily drowning out the sound of its thunderous footfalls as it charges after the bucking stegosaurus.

Both predator and prey barrel down on Roman, and he's almost too stunned to react, feeling detached from reality, like this can't really be happening. His reflexes save him just in time, jinking the snowmobile to the side to prevent the stegosaurus smashing into him with the power of a runaway train. It clomps past, thrashing its tail back and forth like a fish caught in the jaws of a bear. The vicious spikes of its thagomizer swing around and Roman nimbly jumps up onto the seat to avoid his leg being gashed open by the barb of bone as it scrapes down the snowmobile's chassis, ripping off a section of cowling. He watches this in a split second of awed wonder playing out in slow motion before time speeds up once more.

"Fuck, that was close!" gasps Roman, jerking his head forward again as he drops back into the seat. Blinking snow out of his eyes, he sees he's spoken too soon.

His skis point straight into the waiting jaws of the Tyrannosaurus.

***

A wordless, strangled cry of adrenaline-soaked terror rips up Roman's throat, answered by a colossal echo as the Tyrannosaurus roars—an ear-splitting cacophony like tortured steel beams bending in a collapsing building. The shockwave of sound and spittle slaps Roman in the face, nearly sending him from his seat. Blinded by the oozing globs of saliva, he jinks the snowmobile's handlebars, trying to avoid driving directly down the gullet of the monster. The hot stench of decayed flesh and rotten gore washes over him, followed by the pistol shot *bang* of jaws snapping shut, so close to his ear he flinches. More than jink, he jackknifes the handlebars in reflexive response, leaning hard to his right, away from the sound. The snowmobile lifts off its left ski, and he nearly overbalances making a hard, tight turn, desperate to get clear of the dinosaur's chomping bite.

A hard collision like running into a tree sends him tumbling headfirst over the handlebars. He strikes the tree trunk mass with painful force, his body crumbling as he falls hard on ice, stars dancing across the grey jelly of saliva gloop gumming up his sight. The snowmobile over-revs with a shrill cry, as if protesting poor treatment. Dazed, but his body shocked as if by electricity in its panicked fight for survival, Roman shoots up, ignoring any injuries and tearing the thick mask of Tyrannosaurus spit from his face.

The tree is no longer in front of him. It has moved on, the thick trunk of a leg propelling the Tyrannosaurus after its original prey—the meaty stegosaurus—and ignoring the pathetic morsel that is Roman. Next to him, the snowmobile lies on its side, the towed sled twisted awkwardly like a broken limb. Roman is surprised when he finds all his own limbs intact. Testing each with wary movements, he finds the muscles stiff with lactic acid and shock yet capable of movement.

The engine of the snowmobile still chugs away, rumbling and grumbling in complaint. Taking a step towards it, Roman sways, and he realises he might be hurt after all. His head aches, feeling hollow as a cracked egg, and colourful starbursts pop in his sight, triggered by any movement or even trying too hard to think. He resolves to do little of either, righting the snowmobile by grasping one side of the handlebars and leaning back with his weight dangling. The engine splutters in indignation as the snowmobile heaves over and lands on its skis and treads, bouncing on the suspension, and then huffily conks out, going on strike at the worst possible moment.

Because the Tyrannosaurus has not caught the stegosaurus. Its prey having disappeared into the blizzard, the colossal monster turns, keen on the morsel if denied the feast.

33

Roman feels a hot spray of liquid on the inside of his thigh. His terrified mind scrambles to find a reason even as his hands reach down, afraid of what they'll find. Did the stegosaurus's thagomizer spike catch him a blow after all, unzipping the flesh of his thigh? Perhaps it was cleaved open by the claw of the Tyrannosaurus when he ran into the creature's leg.

With his femoral artery severed, he'll bleed out in moments. And while this will save him a horrifying and torturous death ripped apart by the Tyrannosaurus, his fear tells him he's still keen on living, so he's relieved when he feels no pain to touch the area of his leg, only moistness. He lifts his glove and smells it.

"I've pissed myself," he says in disgust.

It's hardly surprising though. The Tyrannosaurus fixes him with the cold glare of a merciless killer, a detached reptile gaze which sees in Roman only living meat and hot blood. And the dinosaur is so *huge*, its chunky, ridge-browed head held aloft, twenty feet from the ground. Roman gains no solace as it tilts the head forward and low, reducing its height. He knows what this stance means.

The Tyrannosaurus is about to charge.

***

A single step pounds the snow, cracking the icy ground underneath with the massive weight. Another step follows, the long, fat leg swinging forward in a surprisingly deft movement like a giant bird. Another, and then another, each following quicker than the last, until the giant dinosaur is running full pelt at Roman.

Roman isn't running, although he probably should be. Instead, he's frantically fighting to get the snowmobile's reluctant engine to turn over.

"Come on, come on," he says, his attention split between thumbing the starter repeatedly and looking back at the closing monster.

The booming of its colossal tread is like the firing of a battery of artillery, its shrieking roar that of incoming missiles. The death these represent is aimed directly at Roman, and he can't stand the pressure of its focused attention. He swings a leg over and sits astride the seat, his back to the monster. Unable to see it anymore, his concentration is a little more focused, enough at least to realise he's repeating the same mistake, over and over, simply hitting the starter and not adjusting when this alone doesn't work.

"Kill switch," he says, seeing his mistake, the same he'd made another time, because he's an *idiot*.

The bellowing, keening roar is just over his shoulder, the footfalls bearing down on him like a rolling avalanche. He hits the kill switch, then the starter, and the snowmobile comes to life, the tinny whine of its revving like a tiny dog barking at a roaring bear.

But this tiny dog is fast, and now Roman runs, shooting out of reach of the Tyrannosaurus as its hot, foetid breath breathes down his neck.

***

The Tyrannosaurus's frustrated cry is a disembodied voice carried on the wind. It emanates from the blinding whiteness—everywhere and nowhere at once—as does the resonant booming of the dinosaur's heavy footfalls. Both reverberate in the air, making the banks of falling snow shake, the individual crystalline snowflakes trembling as if in terror.

The same can be said for Roman, muscles tense, his body humming like a struck tuning fork. He strains his senses to probe the way forward, but they are dulled by the blizzard, visibility low, and he is forced to slow the snowmobile to a crawl even as he wants to flee at full flight.

Conditions on the ground have become worse, too, the tundra a fragmented web of cracked ice. The snowmobile chugs and burbles as he cautiously guides it through this tangled maze of fissures, some large enough to swallow him whole. It is as if the earth itself has broken under the massive strain, and Roman feels himself coming apart as well, the stress almost too much to bear as the monster looms close, unseen yet omnipresent.

How it remains on his trail is not a mystery to Roman, aware as he is that the Tyrannosaurus is an apex predator without equal. Its sense of sight, smell, and hearing are comparable with modern champions of the animal kingdom.

It can see like an eagle, possibly even piercing the blizzard, and certainly has better eyesight than Roman. He scans around, craning his neck to check the angles, fearing the monster will lunge out of the curtains of white haze at any moment. It could easily get the drop on him, and while its hearing might be hampered and confused by the howling wind—as is Roman's—the dinosaur's earholes are tuned to low-frequency detection, and the grinding tracks of the snowmobile churning the ice are enough of an aural track to trace.

But the worst factor is the smell. If the Tyrannosaurus can find carrion over long distances with the effectiveness of a bloodhound, then following the gasoline stench of the snowmobile's exhaust is no trouble at all. It doesn't help that Roman steers directly into the gale, thus keeping his pursuer downwind and able to smell him. He knows this is a mistake, but he has no choice but to keep heading due south into the face of the wind in the hope of reaching the safety of the mountains.

Time grinds by agonisingly slowly, the danger ever-present, and every nerve in Roman's body screams at him to ignore caution and go faster. It feels like a long time before the blizzard finally starts to ease and he can do so, giving the snowmobile some throttle as he weaves around the worst crevices which appear in the tumultuous chaos of the broken permafrost.

The mountains leap out at him through the thinning snow, massive, rocky-backed beasts with jagged claws and teeth of stone. Their craggy peaks are surprisingly close, looming large and foreboding, casting dark shadows on the tundra. The obscured sun forms halos around their heads, concealing the emotion of their faces. Blank, black silhouettes stare down on Roman in mute judgement.

Moving into their protective shade, Roman feels a wash of relief, as if these great monsters, inert as they are, will protect him. But the flush of warmth he feels in their embrace quickly turns cold on his skin, prickling with goosebumps of anticipation, a sixth sense tingling. The premonition is quickly confirmed, snow upon their slopes trembling as a huge, bestial roar reverberates through the air.

Roman turns. He can see the Tyrannosaurus.
And it can see him.

34

Roman sags in defeat. The huge dinosaur is only several hundred metres away and closing the distance fast in huge strides, splayed feet slapping the ice with loud claps. Head low, eyes fixed on him, it aims its body like a missile.

"Fuck me…" says Roman.

Fed up, and nearly overwhelmed with fatigue, he doesn't have much left to give. Neither does the snowmobile, the fuel gauge near empty. Not enough to outrun the monster for long. He eyes the last remaining jerry can. It's full of fuel but lashed down tight on the sled. It'll take minutes to unload it, fill the tank, and get the vehicle started again.

He doesn't have minutes.

He has seconds.

"If only I had a gun," he laments, annoyed that the likes of Trent would be useful right about now. He sits up straight with a start. "Hold up… a gun!"

He has a gun. It's a flare gun, but a gun nonetheless. It's among the gear stowed on the sled, but he made sure it's easy to get to in an emergency.

And this counts as an emergency.

Dismounting, he goes to the sled and pulls the flare gun free of its case. His fingers are fat and clumsy in his gloves, and he fumbles the unfamiliar device into the snow, the flare cartridges scattering. Dropping to his hands and knees, his vision swims with the sudden movement. His brain feels like it's bouncing around on tight tethers which tug painfully like sprained ligaments. One part of him thinks absently, as if standing back at a great remove, that it must be a concussion as the other half, near insane with terror, scrambles hysterically to find the flares and gun in the powdery snow.

The ground beneath his searching hands quakes with the pounding steps of the rampaging Tyrannosaurus rex. Knowing it's a mistake, but unable to help himself, Roman looks up. The dinosaur spins and proliferates like a kaleidoscope image; even more terrifying for the sense of disorientating vertigo created by the swirling chaos as it bears down on Roman.

His fingers frantically rake the snow. He barely registers the clink of plastic against metal. But his subconsciousness recognises this small clue, and he grasps a pair of objects. He lifts the flare gun and a cartridge, holding them before his face like a Rubix cube he must solve before time runs out. But there is no time. None to calm his breathing, to steady his hand—no time at all before he's ripped limb from limb.

In frustration that he'll die just because he's never fired one of these before, he grabs the gun in both hands and bends it, a child petulantly breaking a toy which frustrates them. The barrel snaps open, and a flicker of memory lights up in Roman's mind, a safety briefing in a stuffy office, with him dozing, yet subconsciously absorbing what needs to happen next.

"Get in there, damn it," he says, still trying to force the issue. But try as he might, he can't seem to line up the cartridge with the breach. It seems a square peg in a round hole, or more accurately, many round holes, his dizzy brain spinning the single breach into six like that of a revolver, and him placing a single bullet into one of these, playing Russian roulette. Only it goes into all of them, and he has no chance of avoiding death. The six snap back into one as he clicks the breach shut.

His thumb is on the hammer, pulling it back as he lifts the gun, raising his head at the same time.

He's staring down the gullet of the Tyrannosaurus. It screams a keening, avian cry of triumph and hunger at him, jaws wide to gulp him down whole.

"Swallow this," says Roman, and fires.

***

The shot doesn't go down its throat as Roman planned. Weak with fatigue, his aim wavers and he shoots the flare up the side of the creature's large head instead. It ricochets off its ridged brow, causing the monster to flinch with the glancing impact, flicking its head to the side.

It's the only thing that saves Roman.

The huge monster stomps past him, its keen eyes following not him but the arcing trail of the flare. It puffs with a burst of brilliant red, washing the snow below with blood. Distracted, the Tyrannosaurus chases this point of fading colour as it drifts to the ground. By the time it reaches the point at which it falls, the flare burns out and the hulking monster is left staring at nothing. Snorting with disgust, it swings its wrecking ball head around to look at Roman accusingly.

He's already reloaded the flare gun, but it feels an impotent weapon, nothing but a toy popgun. The shot down the throat might have some effect, burning its insides. Not a killing blow, though capable of wounding or deterring it. It might be enough, but it's a difficult shot he's already failed once, and that at point blank range. He has no intention of letting it get that close again.

Not that he has much choice in the matter. The Tyrannosaurus lowers its head and charges once more, closing the distance in seconds.

Roman yelps in terror and almost drops the flare gun in fright. He shoves it in his pocket and turns, vaulting onto the snowmobile. The vehicle is idling, ready to take off. His hands are on the handlebars, his thumb on the accelerator. With not enough fuel for a prolonged chase, he can at least widen the gap long enough to perhaps fire another flare, throwing the dinosaur off his tail long enough to refuel. It's all he has, his only chance. He grasps it, the throttle depressed. He darts forward, away from danger.

His heart sings with exhilaration. He's escaping.

But then he is jolted by a terrible force as something takes a hold of him and yanks him backwards.

35

There is a horrific burst of blood which explodes across Roman's vision. There is a tearing sound like ripping fabric. There is the sensation of being hurled through the air, the wind whistling in his ears.

And, finally, there is the thudding impact as he lands, bouncing hard on the ice with the force of striking concrete.

Then there is only darkness as consciousness flees him.

36

The pain wakes him. He hates it at first, the return to sensation a sharp shock, with too much stimulus piercing the foggy grey blur of his rebooting brain. It takes him a long, dragged-out second or two to remember pain means he is alive. Then he falls in love with the agony shooting through him, embracing it as an invigorating force, motivating him to move.

But moving is hard.

His limbs are sluggish to respond, the joints stiff, banged up bones creaking in protest as they're tugged at by torn ligaments. Muscles are bruised masses which don't appreciate blood flow, the sensation like burning irons placed on his skin. It takes him far too long to roll over and push against the frozen ground, aware that time is short, that life is short, and growing shorter unless he does something.

Because he can hear the growling of the Tyrannosaurus.

***

Confusion reigns in Roman's tangled mind, only slowly dissipating as he pieces together what he's seeing. But the pieces are jagged, and don't fit easily with his expectations. The most obvious being that he should be dead, or, at least, being eaten alive.

Instead, the hulking bulk of the dinosaur stands stooped over, mere metres away. Jaws working, head shaking, it looks like a monstrous reptilian dog worrying at a bone. It isn't chewing on Roman, and his relief at this fact is matched only by the oddity of the target of its vicious attention. With the crushing might of the world's most powerful bite, the Tyrannosaurus's teeth rend the chassis of the snowmobile with shrill squeals of tearing metal.

Roman remains on his hands and knees. Transfixed by the awful aura of violence radiating off the colossal reptilian predator, he's too afraid to move, lest he draw the creature's attention. It would be all too easy for the dinosaur to realise its mistake and flick around to bite *him*, tearing his flesh, far softer than metal.

Ragged flaps of the grisly stuff already hang by his sides, torn skin coated in blood. Roman assumes only shock is isolating him from the mind-bending pain which should accompany these wounds, received when the dinosaur bit him on the snowmobile and tossed him aside.

It seems only a matter of time before its curiosity is sated with the snowmobile and it realises there's no tender meat to be extracted from its hard shell. Roman wonders why it can't smell him, smell the blood, but then he sees the ragged puncture marks of teeth in the jerry can, fuel sloshing from the pierced metal. Its vapour rises, clouding around the dinosaur's head, confusing it in a soporific haze and clouding its keen sense of smell.

It also gives Roman an idea.

Before he has time to decide if it's a particularly *good* idea, he reaches into his pocket and grips the flare gun. He pulls it out, cocking the hammer with the same fluid motion, and fires.

***

The sharp pop of the firing pin hitting the back of the cartridge is followed a split second later by a loud *whump* as the sparkling flare shoots across the short distance and enters the cloud of fuel vapour, causing instantaneous combustion. The liquid fuel covering the snowmobile, the ground, and even the Tyrannosaurus ignites as well, multiplying the inferno with a sucking *whoosh* which robs the air of oxygen and coughs black smoke into the sky.

A rapidly expanding fireball of brilliant orange, red, and yellow washes over Roman. He drops flat into the snow and buries his face, hoping for the best. But the heat is immense, and it doesn't ease after the first wave of fire sweeps over him. A crackling sound close to his ears is the first sign something is terribly wrong, followed by the smell of burned blood and singed clothing. The situation dawns on him as the first prickles of excruciating pain stab into his back.

He's on fire.

The panic which overwhelms him is irrelevant, his response automatic, simple, and effective. He rolls over in the snow and smothers the flames with a wet sizzle of rising steam.

Lying on his back, panting hard, he watches the plume of black smoke drifting into the blue sky. The relief of the cool snow on his burned skin is bliss.

But it is short lived. The roar of the nearby conflagration is matched by its bestial equivalent; the monstrous, bellowing cry full of agony and rage. Roman tenses, his skin burning all over again as his adrenaline spikes.

The Tyrannosaurus lives.

37

Roman shoots to his feet, ignoring all injuries, all pain, knowing the remainder of his life is to be counted in seconds but having to at least try to run. He looks back over his shoulder as he takes his first steps, instantly regretting it.

The Tyrannosaurus is a vision from hell. Covered in flickering blue fire which dances across its scaly skin, the flesh beneath runs like wax, oozing as it melts, dripping foulness into the snow. Shuddering all over, the dinosaur throws back its head and shrieks like a distressed bird. Its tail flails with impotent rage and the clawed forelimbs tremble in awful agony as it scratches at nothing, finding no relief from its plight.

The head of the thing is the worst, a burning torch completely consumed by fire after being doused in fuel. Its tongue turns to char, the teeth similarly blackened. The eyeballs sizzle and pop, sickening streams of gunk running from the hollow sockets.

And while it might not be able to see Roman, it doesn't have to. Blundering about blindly, overwhelmed by the terrible torture of fire, the huge dinosaur is a wrecking ball of heavy flesh. Its powerful legs kick, stabbing the air with its long, spear tip claws. Roman jumps to the left and right to avoid the clumsy thrusts of these weapons, his reflexes made sluggish by his own pain and fatigue. The Tyrannosaurus spins wildly, sweeping its fat tail around. This time Roman is too slow and it lands like a rubber mallet in his stomach, throwing him several metres. He lands tumbling in the snow.

The pain in his abdomen is immense, but he rises anyway. The Tyrannosaurus bucks like a wild bronco, its curved back undulating unnaturally as it jumps up and down in distress. Its agonised roaring is a continuous, high-pitched shriek which pierces the eardrums with its intensity. It echoes up the mountains and is amplified there, returning as a mighty rumble.

Roman looks beyond the Tyrannosaurus to the snow on the mountain slopes, shaken loose by the sound. It gathers momentum, shifting in a white wave.

He turns to run as the avalanche rushes his way.

***

Roman's steps are painfully slow as if he's running underwater in a dream. He hauls at his legs with his hands, cursing them for traitors as he trudges through the snow, willing them to move faster. He pushes himself to the limit, ignoring the fatigue which tugs at him, the pain which weighs him down; it doesn't feel like it's going to be enough.

Once again, he makes the mistake of looking back. Already, the avalanche has travelled so far, reaching the base of the mountain, the white wave striking the tundra and rebounding to form a great, blank wall. Against this backdrop, the flaming reptilian behemoth dances and capers like a demon, its form distorted and melting. It's an absurd spectacle, and it's unclear whether the dinosaur knows the avalanche is coming to claim it. Roman suspects it will welcome such a death, an act of mercy. But he cares nothing for its suffering, only his own survival, so despair reigns in his heart as he reaches an obstacle in his path.

A deep fissure in the ice curves like a grin. It is the cruel smile of the tundra itself, finally foiling him and delivering the long-promised death.

"Fuck you," says Roman, not slowing. He runs at it, legs throbbing, heart pounding, and jumps into oblivion, trusting to fate.

***

The roar of the avalanche is deafening in Roman's ears as he strikes the far side of the fissure chest first. The blow drives the meagre remnants of air from his lungs, and he almost falls due to the shock, his fingers momentarily numb, scrambling yet grasping nothing.

Luckily, the cleats of his boots catch on something within the fissure, a jutting shelf of ice to give him purchase. It's enough, but he can't rest, shoving himself up over the slippery lip as the avalanche bears down on him, its primal fury a heavy presence pressing into the back of his skull.

He gains his feet and stumbles a few steps before he's struck by flying snow. Spun around, he sees the tumbling mass of the Tyrannosaurus, no longer burning, just a lump of mangled flesh, already dead, having been struck by the full force of the avalanche.

Roman is far more fortunate, most of the impetus of the avalanche spent as it cascades into the depths of the fissure. The Tyrannosaurus goes with it, disappearing as it is buried in snow.

Some of this snow scours Roman's exposed face like flung grit, and he lifts his gloves to ward it off. His feet slide, his whole body pushed backwards as if by a strong gale. This persists and he is sent tumbling onto his back, where he remains as the last of the avalanche's force is spent.

He's buried in only a fine coating of snow, and as he sits up and brushes this off, he realises he's lucky to be alive.

Only he's not. The snowmobile is gone, and with it all the supplies. His death has only been postponed. He stands up and looks about, marooned in a sea of whiteness.

38

"Fuck this," he says, swaying on his feet, the fatigue overwhelming. His heart is a pendulum in his chest, swinging between hope and despair as he rocks back and forth.

"Yeah, *fuck* this."

His voice cracks with feeling as it passes cracked lips. Everything is too heavy, his limbs fettered with iron, his head a cannonball, too ponderous to hold up with his thin neck. Only his guts feel light. Too light. There is nothing to fill the void inside, no food to anchor him and give him strength to continue. He feels his mind drifting, carried away on the wind to swirl in the crags of the mountains. He wants nothing more than to lie down and let the snow cover him again.

But then he'll never get up again, and the past, with all its isolation, trauma, and suffering will have won, finally claiming his life.

"No, fuck *this*," he growls, clenching his fingers into a fist. He looks up at the mountains, his eyes running along their high bastions. They loom over him, those nearby impossibly tall, their faces sheer. But further along the length of the mountain range their ramparts soar and plunge with peaks and troughs like the pulsing of a heart monitor, deciding if life continues. In the distance his eyes light upon a sight he'd forgotten about, even as it dwelled all this time in his subconscious, a symbol of hope, a means of escape.

The pass between the mountains is open. The meltwater of the snow which once filled it is a gushing river, the wellspring he had seen days ago and pointed himself towards. It's all he has, and perhaps all he needs. His boot crunches in the snow.

It all begins with a single step.

***

He should already be dead. There's so much blood. It coats his clothes with a crackling layer of tinted red frost. Only, the blood isn't his. Neither are the tattered strips, hanging slack down his back and sides, his shredded skin. Rather, it is blood-soaked material.

The backpack of blood.

"It saved me, after all," says Roman, his voice sounding small in the shadow of the huge mountains. He gingerly removes the shoulder straps, his abused limbs complaining with pangs of pain. But he's thankful. It could be so much worse. Holding the bag out before him, hanging limp like a burst balloon, he sees the damage the bite of the Tyrannosaurus did to it, and is keenly aware it should have been his own flesh so cruelly torn.

Not that he doesn't have injuries to worry about. He drops the remains of the bag in the snow and holds his head with his hands, trying to keep a cracked egg together and failing, the goop of his scrambled brain feeling as if it's draining out his ears and nose. The headache is crushing, its all-consuming nature a blessing in a way. It takes his mind off the stinging burns on his back, their pain so intense they make his whole body feel like it's vibrating at a high pitch. Eventually, his throbbing head can't even admit this strong sensation, and it fades into the cold numbness, a gift of the tundra. The cold isn't good though, because it seizes his battered joints, making his ankles and knees swell, each step a torture of stabbing knives in delicate places. It's all so much he nearly forgets how hungry he is.

Nearly.

His stomach growls unpleasantly, pleading at him to feed this pathetic, abused beast he keeps caged inside him. But there are no scraps to throw down the hole, and he is forced to continue through this pain. He decides to play a game with himself, a contest between what will kill him first, starvation or exhaustion. Both seem more likely than the cold because, as he approaches the flowing river of meltwater, he's surprised to find the air less frigid.

At least he won't die of thirst. He shambles forward, all else forgotten for the moment. Falling to his knees by the river, he bends down as if worshipping a god which can sustain life. Because that's exactly what the pure, clear water is capable of, extending his prospects of survival.

He kisses its flowing, crystalline surface in benediction, sucking water through cracked lips to flow down a parched throat. It spreads through him, cool and refreshing, appeasing his guts a little and entering the dehydrated cells of his body, plumping them up. Roman feels fuller for it, inflated with fresh vigour. Most importantly, it lifts his spirits. Staring along the length of the river, he can see clear through the pass. Beyond, the sun shines and there is a promise of something different.

39

Trudging across jagged rock, piercing into the heart of the pass, Roman can hear roaring. At first, he thinks it is just his new companion, the river, gushing furiously from its source. It flows too fast, unsustainable in its overeagerness, relieved to finally be released after aeons spent trapped as ice.

But the sound Roman hears is behind this foreground noise. It is unpleasantly familiar. A chill enters his heart even as the sun warms him enough for him to remove his jacket and gloves. He bundles these protectively in front of him, hugging them like a stuffed toy for emotional support.

And he needs it, because the roaring is that of dinosaurs.

The bellowing calls echo through the pass, multiplying the creatures in Roman's mind until there is a vast pack of them bearing down on him from all sides. He quakes in his boots, and he involuntarily turns to retreat. One look back down through the pass is enough to rule out this possibility.

Through its rocky gateposts, he can see the apocalyptically destroyed tundra beyond, its permafrost shattered in a million places like a colossal pane of broken glass. Huge ravines open and close as if the earth itself is a hungry mouth, consuming everything, and squalling banks of scourging snow swirl like rampaging armies, slicing apart all they find. Whatever subterranean or atmospheric forces of seismic upheaval and climate change act upon that inhospitable place, they have transformed it into a hellish wasteland beyond even its former lethality.

There is no going back.

But, even so, it takes all his courage to turn and walk once more into the mouth of the pass, letting it swallow him, aware that there are dinosaurs somewhere inside.

***

Reaching the high point of the pass, where the river flows directly from the rock, Roman looks out upon what lies beyond, his jaw dropping in shock. He doesn't know what he expected. More tundra perhaps, or mountains stretching into the distance, although either would be a death sentence. At best he hoped for a research station, a cosy building nestled in the snow. Something neutral which measures the weather or tags penguins, with hot food and no one wanting to kill him.

But he never dreamed…

The sun is larger than he's ever seen it, filling half the sky and seeming to push down heavily on the earth below, invading its space with its bulky presence. It shines with an orange redness, rather than white yellow, and the scene below is tinted evenly with this diffused light. Electricity hums audibly in the air, as if the radiation from the star has been turned up.

And it is certainly hot. Roman peels off more of his clothes, covered in a sheen of sweat which shines red like blood in the sun's glare. He stumbles forward down the far slope of the pass in a daze, his boots skidding on a scree of small stones. There is no snow or ice on the ground, or anywhere in sight. That is all behind him.

Instead, what is laid out before his astonished eyes is another world. Stretching off into the infinite distance is an impossible landscape, at least for Antarctica. Patches of dense green jungle dot a sunbaked plain of cracked brown earth, resembling mossy moles on aged, tanned skin. Vast bodies of water, misted over with steam, form kidney-shaped lakes, feeding into each other with river arteries which flow back towards distant hills. Smoke and sulphurous yellow gases rise from truncated, bowled peaks which stand sentinel across the plain, each of them far apart, as if guarding their own territory jealously.

"Volcanoes," breathes Roman in hushed wonder. He walks as if in a daydream, dragging his shed clothes behind him in the dirt. They're clutched only loosely in his hands, and he feels like letting them go, the realm before him so rich with warmth it seems like they'll never be needed again.

Dark splotches at the base of the volcanoes, which he first took to be their shadows, bubble and froth as if boiling, their black surfaces glinting with rainbow patinas like oil spills.

"Tar pits?"

He shakes his head in denial, unable to accept any of this, especially the final feature of this bizarre place. There are dinosaurs.

Listening to their monstrous roaring and bellowing as he climbed through the pass, he knew they'd be there. But not like this. Hundreds, *thousands* of them, crossing the plain; herds of slow-moving herbivores, and carnivores dashing through the trees as single predators or hunting packs. They even fill the sky. Great wingspans tipped with claws are silhouetted against the colossal red orb of the sun. These flying pterodactyls swoop and screech as they dive, long beaks glinting like hunting spears, seeking a meal. Roman ducks into the shadow of a rocky overhang to avoid their attention.

But there are other hunters about, much closer. Near the base of the rocky scree, no more than a hundred metres away, an adolescent Tyrannosaurus stalks a herd of parasaurolophuses. Roman feels the old, tired terror rekindle within him at the sight of the apex predator, even one not fully grown. The parasaurolophuses seem unconcerned. The crests sweeping backwards from their skulls turn as they eye the carnivore lazily. Some even bob their heads down to munch upon tufts of grass growing among the rocks, standing on all fours.

As if annoyed by their contempt, the Tyrannosaurus lopes forward, quickly accelerating. The parasaurolophuses lift their forelimbs and take off, surprisingly nimble and explosively powerful on their hind legs. They dart into the jungle, a barrier which brings the Tyrannosaurus up short.

But this isn't the end of the drama. Because here the predator becomes the prey.

40

Roman watches in astonishment as the Tyrannosaurus disappears, dropping out of sight with a mighty crack of snapping timbers. A great spray of leaves is thrown into the air where it stood a second before. From his vantage point, Roman can see it has fallen into a huge hole. But not just any hole. A trap, the branches and leaves carefully placed there to conceal the hole. The implications of this makes Roman's mind swirl as his heart beats faster.

The Tyrannosaurus rages in frantic frenzy, scrabbling to get out, its small forelimbs useless as it scratches at the steep sides of the deep hole. It tries jumping, but it's too bulky and its powerful legs only good for running. There is no escape, the tables turned. The true hunter steps from the shadows of the treeline. Roman's eyes go wide.

They are human.

***

There's more than a dozen of them. Dressed only in loincloths, their skin smeared with earthy pigments of red and brown, they look like cavemen. Only, they are not all men. There are women, too.

Roman's eyes bulge out of their sockets to see them. They wear loincloths as well, but their breasts are exposed, and Roman feels something long dormant within him swell, a great surge of sensation which spreads throughout his body and settles in his groin, pulling at it like a heavy weight. All these years isolated at the base, with only men for company and all hope of returning to the regular world fading, he had given up on ever seeing a woman again. Now they stand before him in a form so visceral and raw, near naked and primal, that he almost goes mad.

Raising a hand of grasping longing, he takes a shuffling step forward, croaking hoarsely like a stepped-on frog, giving wordless expression to years of frustration. The hunters don't hear him.

They raise a cry of triumph as one, lifting long shafts of wood capped with triangular stone spear tips.

The Tyrannosaurus roars, not in anger or defiance, but in bestial terror. Its eyes roll in their sockets like those of cattle being led to the slaughter, aware of their fate. The Tyrannosaurus, too, knows what is next. Perhaps this is what happened to its parents, leaving it all alone in the world so young, to hunt in a world of hunters, where everything is a meal, including itself.

And this is the humans' intention as they stand on the edge of the hole. They don't abandon the beast to die slowly in the hole, ridding their lands of a violent pest. They stab down with their long spears, butchering it, a task they must have repeated many times, such is their skill at delivering quick death to such a large beast. Roman marvels at their efficiency, for they are already jumping down into the hole, taking with them leather sacks and stone knives.

But they don't hack at the flesh, carving Tyrannosaurus steaks to take home and cook. They stab the knives into the neck and chest, and blood flows forth in gushing streams which they catch with the leather containers, smiling and chatting amiably among themselves as they do so.

Roman gawps at the scene. They're harvesting the blood.

***

The men and women not only fill the sacks but place their faces before the squirting streams of blood, letting it flow into their open mouths like water from a drinking fountain. Laughing, they smack their lips happily.

"They're drinking it," says Roman in astonishment, crouching behind a large rock, afraid of being seen by these bloodthirsty savages. He can't help but sneak peeks, though, and he watches as they haul the full sacks of blood out of the hole. Strapping the bulging bladders across their backs with leather thongs, they waddle away like bulbous ticks, having drunk their fill and saving the rest for later.

"What's so special about the blood?" Roman asks himself, his whole life seeming to revolve around that question. Back at the base, draining the stuff from frozen dinosaurs, he had to content himself with never knowing the truth, as much as the mystery plagued him. Now the answer seems tantalisingly close.

He stands from his hiding spot, stumbling and sliding as he descends the rocky slope, the hole like an oasis in the desert, promising not only answers, but succour. His stomach rumbles with the thought of meat, not caring if it's raw.

He's making a racket and throwing up dust, but the savages are gone, disappeared into the jungle, so he doesn't worry, at least not about them. Pterodactyls perch in the crags flanking the pass, their beaks slowly pivoting to point at him as he moves onto the cracked earth of the plain. Roman turns to keep himself facing them, backing up towards the hole. He's so intent on these reptilian birds of prey, and so tired, that he forgets where he's going.

"Oh, shit!" he shouts, his voice shockingly loud in his ears as the ground beneath him gives way. It sets the pterodactyls to flight, swirling around the mountain peaks with flapping wings. But Roman doesn't care about them. He's falling, having tripped into the hole. He lands with a dull thud followed by a wet squelch, bouncing once, twice; first onto the Tyrannosaurus itself and then face down into the bloody mud around it.

"Ugh," says Roman, sitting up and dragging the grotesque gunk from his mouth and eyes. The dead eye of the Tyrannosaurus stares at him, inches from his face, and he flinches. A shadow passes over the hole. He looks up, a pterodactyl momentarily blocking the sun as it flies high overhead. Its shrieking squawk is answered by others out of sight. Roman feels safe from them, for now, sheltered by the hole and the monstrous bulk of the Tyrannosaurus.

He reaches out, running his fingertips across its scaly hide, as if to confirm to himself that it is real. He knows dinosaurs are real, of course, but there is something about this place which makes him think this is all a dream. Touching the scales, though, it all comes slamming home for him.

"The dinosaurs aren't native to the Antarctic tundra," he says, pieces falling rapidly into place. "They're from *here*, wherever here is, and came through the pass the last time it thawed."

Roman doesn't know when that was, but he thinks it must not be so very far in the past. Certainly not millions of years ago. The dinosaurs in the ice revived upon its melting, and so were never dead, but cryogenically frozen by nature, living creatures held in stasis within the ice. Caught unawares by swiftly changing global conditions which snap-froze them, the pendulum of geothermal activity in Antarctica now swings in the opposite direction.

"But this isn't Antarctica," he says, his mind revisiting his memory of the landscape beyond the hole. "This is some other landmass excluded from the maps, one that was never frozen, or at least not recently."

And this much is clear by the nature of the sun in the sky, burning so intensely as to support such massive lifeforms as dinosaurs, and by the abundance of the dinosaurs themselves.

"This place is the real secret, the one worth killing for," he says, punching the Tyrannosaurus in frustration. "But why do this? Why hide the dinosaurs from the world?"

The answer is right in front of him, oozing from the wound in the Tyrannosaurus's neck. Roman gets a weird feeling, as if he's looking at a brightly coloured, poisonous frog, warning him to keep away. His skin is swept with hot flushes, a last vestige of the withdrawals from the gummies, the drug forgotten but the cells of his body remembering, their aching need operating on a level below conscious thought. Roman tries to fight it, feeling as if he's falling into another pit, deeper and darker than the one he's in, or even the metaphorical one he left behind on the tundra, with all the thoughts of suicide.

He presses his lips to the puckering stab wound in the scaly skin, drinking deeply of the life blood of an apex predator.

41

It takes a while for the blood to settle into his roiling guts. He almost vomits it back up, his body rejecting what feels like poison. He forces himself to keep it down, swallowing hard each time his diaphragm pushes the hot gore back up his throat. The taste is awful, reminding him of carnage and death. It goes against every instinct of survival, and while Roman is used to not caring if he lives or dies, after everything he's been through, he *really* wants to live. The blood is the only thing which can save him now.

"If it's good enough for the savages…" he says, not knowing if he means the men and women in loincloths, or whoever it is that's buying this stuff on the other end of the global black market's supply chain. Perhaps it's both, them aware of something he's not. He's determined to find out what it is. The experience feels like the first time he tried drugs, diving into a dark, unknown ocean, hoping something better waits beneath the surface, something more than a regular life.

He falls slack against the wall of the hole. Time passes. His guts are no longer a turbulent ocean. Instead, they are glassy calm, as are his thoughts. His body sings, humming at a high vibration. He's either dying or he's entered a new way of being. There is nothing in between, life exposed as the series of extremes it has always been, pivoting around raw survival.

A shadow passes overhead. Hyperaware, his senses straining, his head darts up to look. He's expecting to see a pterodactyl flying overhead. But the shadow persists, and the shape is all wrong. Roman blinks, repeating cookie cutter silhouettes of gingerbread men stamped along the rim of the hole, surrounding him.

The savages have returned.

***

Not knowing what to do, Roman smiles up at them. They do not smile back, though the blood smeared across each of their lips resembles a smile, grotesque and exaggerated like that of a clown.

Roman laughs nervously. They do not laugh. In the distance a pterodactyl screams. The men and women look up. Roman shifts his weight and stands. The savages take a step back from the hole and point their spears—and their judging eyes—down at him with sharp movements.

The spear tips wave before Roman's eyes like the heads of venomous snakes, ready to strike and kill. Not knowing what else to do, Roman pantomimes the drinking of the blood like some explorer trying to convince a group of cannibals he's one of them.

The savages confer with each other with quick glances. The spears retract. All except one. This is in the hands of a woman, her features feral yet feminine, with intense brown eyes framed by red smeared skin. Roman feels his whole body puff up, swollen by the effects of the blood, thrilled by her attention, even if it's with the intention of killing him.

But the deathblow doesn't come. The spear weaves around his head as if imparting a blessing or testing his courage. When he doesn't flinch or back down, the spear is withdrawn and the savages once more confer, this time in words. Their language is a strange mix of many world languages, leaving Roman wondering who has come through the pass before him, and when.

It's impossible for him to discern their meaning, but when they're done the woman's spear is shoved back into the hole. Only this time it is the wooden haft which is offered to him rather than the stone blade. One of the men barks a single word. Once again, Roman doesn't understand, but can feel its impetus toward action, an order he's being given. He grips the spear's handle firmly, and the woman, hauling with straining, sinewy muscles, pulls him from the hole. Roman stands there, looking at her, and she at him. He feels the dinosaur blood flowing through his body like an elixir of life, removing pain and repairing wounds. It gives him strength and vitality, his body swelling, making him more of a man than he's ever been.

The woman reaches forward. Before Roman can move away, she grabs him by the groin and squeezes hard, all the while staring deep into his eyes. Roman meets the gaze, fighting down the urge to flinch, to pull back, to make even the most miniscule of movements. The moment seems to last a long time, but eventually the woman lets go. She grunts appreciatively with a stiff nod of approval. Her spear still clutched in one hand, she extends the other to Roman, who takes it. Her hand feels warm and inviting, if not soft and uncalloused.

As she leads him away, the rest of the savages close around them. A man begins singing a bizarre, lilting melody. The others join in. Soon even Roman is humming along, not knowing the words but able to follow the simple string of notes. A small leather waterskin is passed around in celebration. It is not filled with water, nor wine. It is blood, and Roman drinks gratefully. He smiles as he smears the excess across his lips with his hand, feeling like he finally knows the secret of it all.

Overhead, the pterodactyls shriek and circle, but the savages keep them at bay with threatening stabs into the air. In the distance, other dinosaurs call and honk, roar and snarl, a whole world of threatening monsters. But as he enters the jungle to begin a new life, Roman feels no fear.

In fact, he's never felt so alive.

SEVEREDPRESS

facebook.com/severedpress
twitter.com/severedpress

CHECK OUT OTHER GREAT DINOSAUR THRILLERS

JURASSIC ISLAND
by Viktor Zarkov

Guided by satellite photos and modern technology a ragtag group of survivalists and scientists travel to an uncharted island in the remote South Indian Ocean. Things go to hell in a hurry once the team reaches the island and the massive megalodon that attacked their boats is only the beginning of their desperate fight for survival.

Nothing could have prepared billionaire explorer Joseph Thornton and washed up archaeologist Christopher "Colt" McKinnon for the terrifying prehistoric creatures that wait for them on JURASSIC ISLAND!

K-REX
by L.Z. Hunter

Deep within the Congo jungle, Circuitz Mining employs mercenaries as security for its Coltan mining site. Armed with assault rifles and decades of experience, nothing should go wrong. However, the dangers within the jungle stretch beyond venomous snakes and poisonous spiders. There is more to fear than guerrillas and vicious animals. Undetected, something lurks under the expansive treetop canopy . . .

Something ancient.

Something dangerous.

Kasai Rex!

SEVEREDPRESS

facebook.com/severedpress
twitter.com/severedpress

CHECK OUT OTHER GREAT DINOSAUR THRILLERS

SPINOSAURUS
by Hugo Navikov

Brett Russell is a hunter of the rarest game. His targets are cryptids, animals denied by science. But they are well known by those living on the edges of civilization, where monsters attack and devour their animals and children and lay ruin to their shantytowns.
When a shadowy organization sends Brett to the Congo in search of the legendary dinosaur cryptid Kasai Rex, he will face much more than a terrifying monster from the past.
Spinosaurus is a dinosaur thriller packed with intrigue, action and giant prehistoric predators.

LAND OF DEATH
by Eric S Brown & Alex Laybourne

A group of American soldiers, fleeing an organized attack on their base camp in the Middle East, encounter a storm unlike anything they've seen before. When the storm subsides, they wake up to find themselves no longer in the desert and perhaps not even on Earth. The jungle they've been deposited in is a place ruled by prehistoric creatures long extinct. Each day is a struggle to survive as their ammo begins to run low and virtually everything they encounter, in this land they've been hurled into, is a deadly threat.

SEVEREDPRESS

facebook.com/severedpress
twitter.com/severedpress

CHECK OUT OTHER GREAT DINOSAUR THRILLERS

WRITTEN IN STONE
by David Rhodes

Charles Dawson is trapped 100 million years in the past. Trying to survive from day to day in a world of dinosaurs he devises a plan to change his fate. As he begins to write messages in the soft mud of a nearby stream, he can only hope they will be found by someone who can stop his time travel. Professor Ron Fontana and Professor Ray Taggit, scientists with opposing views, each discover the fossilized messages. While attempting to save Charles, Professor Fontana, his daughter Lauren and their friend Danny are forced to join Taggit and his group of mercenaries. Taggit does not intend to rescue Charles Dawson, but to force Dawson to travel back in time to gather samples for Taggit's fame and fortune. As the two groups jump through time they find they must work together to make it back alive as this fast-paced thriller climaxes at the very moment the age of dinosaurs is ending.

HARD TIME
by Alex Laybourne

Rookie officer Peter Malone and his heavily armed team are sent on a deadly mission to extract a dangerous criminal from a classified prison world. A Kruger Correctional facility where only the hardest, most vicious criminals are sent to fend for themselves, never to return.

But when the team come face to face with ancient beasts from a lost world, their mission is changed. The new objective: Survive.